I0682366

Insatiable Trysts
Sexy Stories Collection

VOLUME 13

20 EROTIC SHORT STORIES

CHARA GLADEY

Insatiable Trysts/ Chara Gladey. – 2nd ed.
Xplicit Press, an imprint of TLM Media LLC

ISBN-13: 978-1-62327-635-5
ISBN-10: 1-62327-635-7
eISBN: 978-1-62327-636-2

Printed in the United States of America

CONTENTS

CONTENTS

1 BOG MAN I:
SIOBHAN'S FANTASY

Fuck this weather, really. Fuck it! Can't it ever do any better than this in Ireland? Does it have to fucking rain all the time?

Siobhan opened her eyes in bed. The room, with its stone and white plaster walls, was freezing. It must have been nine o'clock or later, yet it was grey and dark outside the little window, as if there would be no daylight at all.

A conveniently sized dildo was warm and rolling in bed between her bare thighs. Siobhan felt a little embarrassed that she had resorted to the toy last night. After her usual long and lonely drive west from Cork yesterday, in her battered Irish-green French Citroen deux chevaux, the hot-blooded woman had been as horny as hell. With the wind howling outside and the aromatic peat and coal fire burning hard in the little grate to warm the place, Siobhan had shone the little bedside light on herself.

It was cold, but Siobhan never wore anything to bed, regardless of the temperature. In front of the faded old full-length mirror in her weekend cottage, as usual, she enjoyed slowly removing her gear. First, the toasty thick cashmere jumper and then the woolen skirt dropped to the floor. Then her full shapely body stood gloriously there, shining forth, spots of freckles blooming freely everywhere. As always, she caught her breath when she looked at the bright red tuff of pubic hair which formed an island in the middle of her thick soft thighs.

This cunt has given her so much pleasure over her years. Really, there was hardly a night or day when that naughty place has not sent her wild. Her right hand went down to it again, almost automatically, and she kneaded her forested mound firmly, groaning. Her deft index finger went straight to her secret tender valley in the middle of that bushy mound. The practiced finger was already on her firm little button of a clitoris, which hardened as she rubbed. In this horny kind of mood, Siobhan knew that she would not last long until she exploded.

As the practiced flicking and rubbing of her fingers continued and picked up speed, the young woman in the mirror rocked back and forth, her pelvis pushing forward and her thighs opening more. The small bedroom filled with the scent rising from her warm cunt. That sexy aroma never failed to arouse her.

"Shit... shit... shit. Fuck... fuck... fuck," was all she could manage to blubber. Siobhan's long red hair now obscured her vision as it flopped back and forth in front of her face. She saw very little now through the hair in her mounting excitement. Her tight vagina was gripping her whole body, and squeezed even more tightly as she rubbed her throbbing pink clit.

"Aghhhhhhhhhhhhhhhhhhhhhh!" screamed Siobhan loudly at her highest point before a shuddering and crashing release. Her piercing scream could have been heard in the empty dark countryside for miles around, if there had been anyone silly enough to have been out there. Flopping into the freezing bed a little later, the incorrigible girl was ready for another such orgasm as her general deep yearning was still not at all sated that night.

She had then skipped naked through the dark house to the fridge and brought out the chilled cucumber. When she slid it into her wet vagina later in bed, it felt like the many hard penises that her always-hungry hole had embraced and swallowed in its many torrid encounters so far.

This morning Siobhan rose, her naked body still radiating warmth from her bed. It was her weekend of freedom, so she had decided to spend it naked. There was plenty of peat to stoke the fire up to heat the freezing cottage a little more.

The rain had stopped. In the grey-green damp bog, a strong young man was cutting peat, digging it up to dry in dark-brown mounds on the ground.

Siobhan had admired him before from her upstairs bedroom window on other weekends. Now she used her binoculars to study him closer. He was quite something, she concluded, and he made the tender area between her legs moist.

She could imagine his white, muscular buttocks under his grey work trousers, and what was bulging in front of them. The naked woman looked at her crumpled bed and back to the boy. Somehow, she would get him in that bed. She wasn't sure how, but she knew she needed him, and fast.

She decided she'd better put some clothes on, despite her vow of weekend nakedness, if only to have him take them off later. As she left through the kitchen's back door, bright sunshine touched the girl's face, warming the chill blown from the nearby ocean. The dear old stone cottage, built in the traditional Irish country architecture, stood alone, white and lonely, in the vast and empty countryside. Ballinskelligs Bay, with its white ring of a beach, was visible far in the distance, right against the dominating slope of a mountain range, covered with thick trees.

Siobhan simply loved it there.

"Hi there. I'm Siobhan. How're yer?" said the girl.

"Hi. I'm Billy. Am just grand, and you," answered the boy.

"Am grand too, tanks," said Siobhan. "Say, if you feel like a break from your work, I can give you some buttered toasts and a cup of hot tea? How would that be?"

"That would grand," he said, smiling now. "Wouldn't say no to a cupper right now." His russet hair showed through from under his work beanie.

"Actually, I also need a little help with the plumbing," said Siobhan, smiling sweetly.

The man thrust his peat-cutting spade hard into the ground, and together they walked back to the cottage.

The young man looked at her through the steam of a big mug of tea, while munching on buttered toast with strawberry jam. Siobhan shivered as she thought about what his handsome face would like as he came. She knew it was now or never. "The kitchen sink drain is leaking. Could you tighten it up for me?" asked Siobhan, handing him a toolbox.

The boy immediately knelt down to tighten the pipe joint under the sink. Of course, Siobhan herself had loosened the joint before inviting him over. As the boy glanced up at her from his work, Siobhan ever so casually moved her knees apart so that the boy had a clear view right to the tops of her legs. She wore no panties under her short black skirt.

The look on the boy's face was priceless. He could not take his eyes off the red bush of a target that had been put in front of him. Surprising herself, her heart beating rapidly, Siobhan stared directly back at the man, smiling slightly.

As her bog man sat back on the cold kitchen floor, Siobhan made her move.

Again, still wondering about her own audacity, Siobhan slowly lifted the front of her short woolen skirt so that her cunt hairs brushed the boy's surprised face. Her strong, alluring smell rose from her moist muff.

"How's that for an invitation that you didn't expect," she asked, smiling. The young man couldn't even speak, so entranced was he by her scent and heat.

The woman squatted down on the poor man's muscular thighs. The large bulge under the zip of his soiled and smelly corduroy work trousers seemed to be waiting for her to unzip it – luckily, it didn't have to wait too long. Siobhan's anxious hands freed the thick pale-pink penis, which sprang to attention instantly under her sexual ministrations. The woman's soft pink mouth seemed to automatically descend onto the angry bulge of the head, barely fitting it into her hungry mouth. Siobhan's moist tongue licked it clean, preparing it for its next task.

"Jesus, Mary and Joseph," mumbled the woman as she aimed the solid rod at the entrance of her vagina, hesitating to sit down on it because of its sheer size.

"You are a very big boy, Billy," she mumbled further. Billy himself still had a stunned look on his face.

"Jesus, Jesus," screamed Siobhan as she

let his towering penis push deep into her. "That is something fierce!" She wondered if she'd even survive this monster cock.

Siobhan gave Billy a quick, sloppy kiss on the mouth in her hurry to start riding him. Using his solid shoulders as support, her hungry cunt rode her man, making indecent sloshing sounds as their bodies met.

"Where have you been all of my life, Billy?" Siobhan tried to plant a kiss on him again, but missed as they rutted faster.

"I've been 'ere... waiting for yer, I guess," says Billy finally, with a wry smile.

Siobhan could feel herself riding up a mountain, poised at the precipice, almost terrified of the release she craved.

Billy, too, was wriggling, heaving and breathing hard. Just at the point of Siobhan's own shuddering peak, she felt her internal canal filled with the sudden heat of Billy's sperms. A long and loud scream once again reverberated into the lonely and indifferent bog.

2 BOG MAN II:
INSATIABLE SIOBHAN

Siobhan's bog man wanted to go out to finish his work cutting peat for the day, even after Siobhan had seduced him into an energy-draining fuck on the cold kitchen floor. Not that Billy had had much of a choice in the matter: he was practically raped by this voracious young woman, who craved sex like a fat boy craves candy.

Siobhan had not felt this happy for a long time, as she lay in her warm bed next to a delicious hunk of an Irish lad, who was all hers for now.

The young woman thought of last weekend when she had first lured her farm boy to the cottage from his hard work in the field. After she had ridden him joyfully on the kitchen floor, it took a bit of persuading to stop the conscientious lad from going out again to cut more peat in the fading light.

Instead, Siobhan was able to somehow pull him up by his hand upstairs into the bedroom. There was no stopping her stallion then.

It was his turn to mount her. While admiring the fading evening outside from the little window, the young woman's full breasts were grabbed from behind by steel-like strong hands that had delved under her pullover. Then without a word, the willing woman was pushed unceremoniously on to the soft bed on her front and her skirt quickly was lifted to expose her full round ass, bare and very vulnerable.

With her heart pumping, she held her breath while Billy threw off his clothes. What was this man going do to her in this position? Her answer soon came, as Billy's penis nosed between her legs. No, he is not going to do that, Siobhan thought. But he definitely was.

"Oh, Jesus," she screamed, "Jesus, Mary and Joseph!"

Billy's rod had pushed into her anus. Rarely had she allowed any of her men to do that to her. She thought of stopping this man but couldn't: it felt too good.

"Where did you learn to do that, Billy?" she mumbled, her face pressed into the bed.

The sensation was raw, with some pain, as her intruder was not too well lubricated. "Ah, fuck, Billy, go easy!"

Then her man was on the move, his rock-hard penis sliding in and out deep in her ass. For Siobhan, orgasms were the biggest blessing God had given her. With her face buried in the bed, and the weight of Billy's muscular body on her back, Siobhan was ready once again to be overwhelmed.

"Oh hell, Billy, fucking hell hole," she screamed. Then she heard the first animal cry from her bog man, as he plunged all the way into her poor hole and emptied another long, big load of warm semen into her.

"I'll take you to meet my folks," said Billy over his full Irish breakfast of sausages, bacon, eggs and tomatoes that Siobhan had cooked for him.

Billy's farm was a fairly long walk from Siobhan's beautiful cottage, but she loved the countryside, with its sun-dappled hills that always smelled vaguely of the nearby ocean. The walk was pleasant, and soon enough, they reached Billy's family farm.

Billy's elderly parents were busy working, tending to the livestock and crops that were their livelihood. So as not to disturb them, Billy grabbed Siobhan's hand and led her quietly to his "secret place": a hayloft on the edge of the small property.

Once they reached the loft, they stripped naked without having to say a word about it, for it just seemed like the thing to do.

Naked and pink like two farm animals, the new lovers laughed and crawled on all fours over to the side of the opening in the loft, where they could see the farmhouse and the garden where Billy's parents worked. Stallion Billy was not slow to react to Siobhan Mare's proffered behind - delectably round, with a dainty puckered anus and an alarmingly red bushy cunt.

He mounted her quickly, thrusting into her waiting vagina. But the bog animal still took his time – as he thrust, he began groping her firm, white breasts, flicking her pert nipples, traveling down to her thick bush to tug at her hairs, then gravitating back to her mounds to begin the journey again. Siobhan knew she would let him shove his long animal penis into her all day long; she couldn't think of a better way to spend such a day.

Just as Siobhan felt yet another mind-blowing orgasm approach, her man slipped out of her!

"Hey, Billy, where did you go?" she whispered, trying to not to make too much noise.

Billy flipped her over none too gently spread her thighs roughly apart. His long rod ploughed deeply into her from the front, provoking a loud moan.

"Jesus Christ," screamed Siobhan, despite her attempt to keep quiet. Again, her wonderful man brought her to a writhing peak. But this time, it was Siobhan who grabbed his penis out of her cunt, deftly sliding her body down on the hay to put her mouth on the throbbing hot dick.

"Oh, girl!" blurted Billy, "fucking hell!" as an alarming amount of hot sperm puffed out her smooth cheeks.

"I needed that lunch," she said to her man with a wide smile.

"Good show, you two!" Siobhan gasped at the sound of Billy's parents clapping from the corner.

"Hi, Dad," said Billy, not at all surprised.

Both his mum and dad were sitting comfortably on the soft hay in the far corner near the top of the ladder.

"Hi, Mr. and Mrs. Moran," stammered Siobhan, not at all sure how to handle all this.

The old couple slowly rose and walked over to the sweaty couple, bright smiles illuminating their wrinkled faces.

Mary Moran gently handed Siobhan her clothes and gave her a little hug.

"When you are ready, come down, dear," she said. "I have a nice hot Irish stew cooking in the pot. Don't you lovebirds hurry, though! Patrick and I know all about what goes on up here. *We* even used to have some fun up here, back when we could do such things."

"Who says we can't now, dearie," said old Patrick with a wicked glint in his eyes. "I'll show you tonight!"

3 AHMED'S ANGEL

"**W**elcome to wild West Virginia," the road sign says.

"Thank you," says Ahmed out loud to himself in the car. "I am indeed happy to be here."

The road ahead is empty. The Skyline Drive of his map is taking him and his American beauty up and up into the Blue Ridge Mountains, ablaze with incredible autumnal colors of the forest trees. A perfect present for his birthday today.

It's November and "fall", as he has learned well in his English class. Brilliant gold copper leaves are carpeting both sides of the highway, and he swerves his swanky old Cadillac here and there to send the leaves into the air, scattering upward, and then tumbling back beautifully once again.

Yes, HIS car.

Allah be praised for his uncle. Rich with

his petrol money, that man whom Ahmed loves, and to whom Ahmed is a favorite nephew, has simply wired money into his account as a surprise birthday present last week.

Ahmed was off in a flash down the road to the used-car yard where, on his daily walk to school, he has admired the silver-and-blue old Cadillac that looks like a flat spaceship has landed there by mistake, and has been captured.

What a machine. What a birthday present.

Ahead it's getting dark and some early stars are already twinkling through the canopy of golden leaves.

There is a figure on the road, hitchhiking.

Our student is in a quandary. This is his first drive in this country and maybe he shouldn't expose anyone to risks. And this also looks like a hippie girl.

Yet his was the only car on the road and it was getting dark and unsafe for the girl alone. He drives past slowly but finally stops some distance past.

The girl runs over and opens the door.

"Thank you so much," she says. "I was afraid that it was going to be a long wait in the dark."

"Er ... I ...am...happy to...stop," replies Ahmed slowly, searching for words.

"Hi, I'm Jane. You're cute," says the young girl, her long blond hair framing a face so beautiful it stuns Ahmed.

"So ... pretty!" whispers Ahmed, to himself mainly, while concentrating on pulling back onto the road. "Hello. I...am...Ahmed." He turns to shake her hand.

"You foreign, or something?," asks Jane with the prettiest smile.

"I...come...from...Iraq."

"Wow, I don't know any Iraquians," says the girl.

"We...say...Iraqi," Ahmed says.

"Whatever! Hey, cute Ira-qi, can I buy you a take-out in return for my lift? Stop at this place up the road?"

"Take-out?"

"Yeah, take-out. Ya know, yummy food."

With their hot fries in hand, Jane tells Ahmed to turn to a lonely lookout way off the main road where they eat silently, looking out to some lights on the plain below.

Ahmed at first refuses an offered can of beer, but Jane insists.

"Warm night, eh?" says Jane after some time, and turns to face him as she begins to undress, taking her leather vest then shirt off to reveal her small pert breasts with their erect pink nipples.

"What...you...do...?," stammers Ahmed.

"What I do is taking my clothes off, for the night Why don't you do too?" She looks at him and smiles.

"There is no one around except deer, so we can bunk here. You got a big comfy back seat."

"Bunk?..."

"Yeah, sleep, and fuck!," says Jane.

"Fuck?"

"Yeah, fuck. A nice strong boy like you would want that, wouldn't you, before bed?," she says, "I haven't had a decent fuck for at least a week and I am one horny girl!"

"Hor...ny?"

As she rattles on, Jane strips and is now gloriously naked and a mixture of her body smells fills the cab. Her pubic hair is as golden blond as her swinging hair.

"Your turn," she says and starts to unbutton Ahmed's shirt. He doesn't stop her but leans back his seat.

"That's better," says Jane.

Ahmed can't say to this ministering angel that this is shaping up to be the best birthday present ever, even better than the car.

But he himself doesn't understand this culture. Why would a woman simply do this?

He helps her now to remove his trousers but keeps his undies on.

Quick as a flash his angel climbs on him and her cunt presses his dark hard cock whose thick shiny head has escaped well out of his briefs.

As it's all happening directly in front of him, Ahmed is overwhelmed by the sight. His blond angel is rubbing her full mound on the trunk of his penis. She begins slowly at first, then faster.

Some convenient slickness has come out to her vagina to oil the sliding of her cunt.

"You've got quite a weapon there, Buddy," mumbles Jane now. "A real weapon of mass destruction. And it's going to destroy me soon, I can feel it."

Ahmed can see clearly his angel's pink clitoris growing between the open crack with a drift of lovely hair the color of the golden autumn leaves on either side.

He is fascinated by the shape of this lovely button that seems to have a life of its own. It also seems to be sending his angel wilder. He sees that when the wet button presses down on the shaft of his dick, the lovely young woman growls and tosses hair backward and forward.

With his thumb, he tentatively touches the button and feels its hardness.

"Oh, fucking hell, don't stop," growls his angel, so Ahmed presses and caresses the magic spot faster and more firmly with his thumb.

Ahmed thinks that he needs to hang on, and not disgrace his manhood by shooting off too early.

His woman's spectacular long golden thighs are all wide open in front of him now. Her lovely body is arched back, pointing her wonderful breasts skyward. What a sight.

She is pushing down much harder on the shaft of his cock now then lets out a shrill, un-angel-like scream into the quiet night.

As if to finish off both of them, Jane now holds his long wet prick to stand up then quickly impales herself on it.

Again Ahmed has never felt such sensation of his penis being enveloped totally by soft flesh. It's like it has found its way back home to a place it should never have strayed from in the first place.

It's never like this when he uses his own hand.

As the angel's vagina grips and strokes his shaft, and the spectacular view of the woman savoring her ride on his cock, Ahmed hangs on to the car seat more then also pushes up his cock in time to her movements up and down.

But he can't hang on that much longer. Thankfully his angel explodes again now, her face grimacing with extreme pleasure and unearthly sounds come out of her lovely full mouth.

The student, having learned a lot, can let himself go now, like a rocket or firecrackers going up in a huge way. It is as if some part of himself down there has shot up to impregnate his angel.

"This is fuck...ing?" he asks, catching his breath.

"This is fucking, and you fuck very well, my Iraqi Buddy," says Jane. "Let me be your English teacher anytime. In fact, as soon as you grab some strength back, we can have another lesson.

"You have worn me out, Buddy Boy," says Jane giving Ahmed his first full kiss from a woman.

The two get themselves ready to spend the night together. Ahmed walks out on the cold grass into the fine night, relishing being naked. Also bare, Jane has run after him on tiptoes and catches him with a tight hug from behind. "Weeeee," she sings.

Ahmed's angel dances around on the soft grass like a ballet dancer now, but wilder, pirouetting with her arms and legs sweeping gracefully in the night air.

"Come here, Ahmed," she calls for him to follow to the forest edge. It's the first time the girl has tried to call him by name. "I'm a tree-hugger, see, and I'll hug this little trunk and you fuck me from behind. How's that?"

"Fuck...behind...OK!" stammers Ahmed.

The sight of Jane's lovely full bum pushed back to him with her round thighs slightly apart is the stuff of wet dreams to Ahmed.

His ever-ready cock is as hard again as a stick of wood and is pointing to the target of blond bush presented to it. Deciding, he quickly chose her lower hole, not wanting to cause her pain, although he prefers the top tighter opening.

"Fuck me good, Ahmed, fuck me good, man!" yells Jane.

Again Ahmed's tool has speared into a place that it belongs. Under the weak starlight, the two lovers push and shove each other, at first leisurely then faster and faster, as new animal noises rise to startle any deer or raccoon in the vicinity.

Just as Ahmed shoots long into his jiggling target and collapses on top of his screaming angel, a bright flash of car headlight sweep right by them, fortunately missing the struggling lovers.

"Shit!", whispers Jane. "Get down, buddy!"

With his penis still inside Jane, the two drop to the dewy leaves on the rough ground behind some low thick bushes.

A big old pick-up trucks with big wheel

rolls in to park in front of Ahmed's car. The partial silhouettes of three men step out, one of them carrying a long hunting rifle with a silencer attached.

The horns of a stag can be seen sticking out from the back of the truck.

With the truck's bank of bright lights illuminating forest trees, the men opened the front doors of the Cadillac.

"Shit, and double shit, the key is still in the ignition," whispers Jane.

"Nice car," says the burly guy with the rifle.

"A bit of an old bomb," says another who then shines his torch light all around, sweeping past the bushes that the lovers are hiding behind, still attached.

The men climb back into their truck and it roars away.

That birthday night Ahmed spends asleep between his angel's hospitable thighs on the big back seat of his American dream machine.

Earlier, while cuddled together under a blanket, his angel had asked him to marry her and stay in the mountains with her forever in her log cabin. She promised unlimited English and sex lessons.

Ahmed grabs this other birthday present with both of his grateful hands.

4 MIKO'S SNOW RIDE

Japanese travelers in America, Miko splits up with her boyfriend Hiyuwaki and takes a bus north while traveling to Alaska. She has a comfortable sexual meeting on the Greyhound bus with a kind older American man while traveling through Montana, and they decide to take a night's break together in a motel en route.

The bus is quiet with all the passengers deep in sleep. A man snores way up the front. But Miko is awake, reliving the fight with her fiancé that has effectively ruined their travels in America. The snow is thick outside on the side of the highway where it looks like the whole world has gone white and frozen.

Miko loves snowy landscapes and always has. Back home in Japan, she loved to travel north in the depth of winter and has, once or twice, followed the snowy wanderings of Basho, the master Haiku poet in history.

Her reclined bus seat is so comfortable on this Greyhound bus. There is a nice old man fast asleep next to her under his blanket, while she is toasty and warm under hers.

Miko feels safe enough to rub herself to sleep now, as she often does in her own bed back home. Her boyfriend Hiyuwaki had that job while they have been on the road. But now, they have painfully split up.

He has taken off in a huff on a southern route, while she decides to follow the song "Up to Alaska" and go there to see it in glorious winter. She hopes to meet her fiancé again somewhere, if he emails.

With her bottom pushed against the arm rest dividing the seats and against the warm bulk of the man's body, Miko's right hand has gone under her underwear and is kneading and rubbing between her legs. She is trying to keep still and not disturb her neighbor, but it's hard. Having an ultra-sensitive cunt, Miko knows that her shuddering crescendo is not far away.

But wait, there is another warm hand now surprisingly feeling the round cheek of her bottom. Miko glances back quickly at the old man, but his head is turned away and his eyes are shut.

But his soft thick right hand has come alive on its own, even when its owner is apparently not awake, and it feels really good as it caresses her bum.

So Miko continues rubbing around her vagina, while the fingers of the visiting hand now crawl around her anus. The girl holds her breath.

The index finger of the hand moves forward to her innermost gateway and doesn't hesitate before pushing right in. Miko shudders and is thankful that her vagina is already moist from her own exploration. With the man's thick finger slipping even further into her hole, Miko tries now to control her rising orgasm, made even stronger now by the stranger's finger sliding in and out of her vagina, like a penis seeking its own satisfaction.

She bites the side of her blanket with her eyes shut, and her body shakes uncontrollably. Recovering some composure, Miko glances anxiously back to the old man, whose face is turned her way now but his eyes remained shut.

Tired now after her arousal, the woman settles back to sleep in the same position, as she didn't really want the man to move his fat finger out of her cunt.

The big bus pulls in quietly now into a gas station that has also a brightly lit and shiny diner. Miko stirs from her long and restful slumber. There is no finger in her cunt anymore.

Instead, she sees her tall big man, with thick wavy and perfectly grey hair, now buying his supper from the serving counter, then finding himself a table in a corner.

Miko buys her favorite combination of fries, burger, and coke, taking care to choose a table well away from the man's table. She is starving.

The old man is still finishing his coffee

CHARA GLADEY

when Miko slips out of the diner's door into the frozen night and quickly back into the warm bus.

She pretends to be asleep curled up when her neighbor returns. Through slits in her closed eyes, she can see him looking at her with eyes that are gentle. His mouth has a trace of a smile.

Off rolls the bus again smoothly into the night. It's still a long way ahead to Alaska from the wilds of Montana, Miko realizes.

As the man settles back under his blanket again, Miko pretends to turn in her sleep to curl up with her head accidentally leaning on the neighbor's shoulder, who seems not to have noticed the move.

"Will he, or won't he?" the woman has been debating with herself. He was bold enough to do it with her. But how would this old man take it in return. Here goes nothing, thinks Miko.

Her right hand is slowly creeping under her own blanket and crosses the border to snake under the neighbor's blanket, then meets with the mountain of his body.

Accompanied by a trembling heart, Miko's hand slides onto the soft large mound of his genitals, under their layers of clothing. Her fingers quickly found the little zipper handle in the folds of his fly. Still no visible reaction from the apparently sleeping man.

The bold woman now slowly open the man's zipper, and her right hand slides in to barely cup the soft bulge in his underwear. That bulge grows larger and hardens alarmingly with the thick penis springing up to stand erect.

Still, no other sign of life from the old man.

As Miko has done countless times for her fiancé's smaller dick, she squeezes the hard penis now and stokes it. The man's body stirs in response, and his head moves but his eyes are still firmly shut. Looking across the man's bulk under the blanket through the window opposite, snow is beautiful in the bright night.

His long rod in her grip is a hard stick of muscle now. Miko also sniffs a strong erotic scent coming all the way from under the blanket. She hasn't been stroking him long and is very much enjoying the feel of it all, when her hands tell her to prepare for his ejaculation.

The thoughtful woman has kept the soft paper towels handed out with her burger. Now, she pushes the tissue paper under the blankets to cover the hot bulb end of the man's cock.

Just in time too, as the penis agitates to shoot out a veritable waterfall of hot sperm while the man's body stiffens and trembles a couple of times.

An attractive older woman, asleep in the next seat across the aisle, stirs and looks in their direction. She sees an old man with a small pretty Asian girl asleep with her head leaning on his shoulder.

The man's left hand now moves under the blanket and helps Miko's hand to dry the tip of the soaked penis, then takes the tissues away. A strong smell of semen now rises into the compartment of the sleeping bus. Miko feels sure that the suspicious woman passenger who has woken up can smell it too.

With his eyes still closed, the old man turns so that his bulky body and his head touch the top of hers. His strong left hand now slips under their blankets, and deftly goes under her pullover and bras to cup her right bare breast.

"Thank you," he whispers quietly in Miko's ear, as the bus lulls them both to sleep once again. When Miko wakes, dawn is breaking over the hills. Snow is even thicker here, and the bus has to drive over patches of it on the road.

Her old man is still asleep beside her, but his big hand is no longer on her bare breast but is neatly cupped on her bare cunt under the blanket. How long it has been there and what it has been up to when she was asleep, goodness only knows.

Sunlight wakes the man up now.

"Hi, we haven't met. I'm Dan," says the man with a kind smile, while pulling his hand back away from her cunt without any embarrassment.

"Hello, I'm Miko," she says shyly.

"Thanks for last night. You were an angel," Dan says. "May I be very forward and make an indecent proposal?"

"Yes," says Miko quietly, who doesn't know how else to respond.

"I'm on my way home to Alaska, so a long way to go yet, and I have been on buses for days. So I thought I would take a break here in Livingston this morning and spend a night in a motel, then catch a bus to Seattle tomorrow."

"Would you stop here with me and keep me company?" Dan asks. His eyes are kind. "Yes, because I am going to Alaska too," says Miko without hesitation. She doesn't know why she did that.

She is furiously recalling the horrific films of serial murders and mutilations, even using a chainsaw, which apparently go on in small-town America. Dan doesn't look like a serial killer, but she will be alone in a motel room with him in the middle of absolutely nowhere.

After their big fried breakfasts, Dan checks them in to an old motel on the main road, covered with snow and sparkling icicles which unfortunately reminds Miko of the motel in the movie Psycho.

The man at reception scrutinizes them when Dan signs them in as Mr. and Mrs. Dan Smyth. He does not look like Anthony Perkins.

The piping hot shower revitalizes Miko. But just when she is ready to come out of it, Dan knocks on the bathroom door and asks if he can come in.

Again, Miko finds herself saying yes. Can she never refuse this man?

Under the steaming shower together, the hulk of a man with his big muscles and a beer belly covered with gold and grey hair, at first, soaps himself then all over the small and shapely body of Miko.

"You have a stunning body," says Dan as

his big strong hands soap her everywhere.

Bright sun is shining in through the far window as Dan guides Miko to lie on her back on the bed. Then she lets him spread her thighs wide so that her full mound of Venus, covered with thick black hair, lays split apart.

Miko shudders at the size and length of this man's cock that is now forcing itself into her tight opening, backed by his full weight that is now heavy on her.

Hiyuwaki flashes a protest in her mind but then she abandons herself, arms overhead, to be fully plowed by this huffing American man.

5 BEST FRIEND WEEKEND

"What exactly do you want to do this weekend?" Laura's best friend Sean asks her.

He has come into her room to listen to some new CDs that she has bought on her recent trip to New York, using her new swanky head phones.

"We are 19 and we've never fucked each other." replies the vivacious Laura.

"What's wrong with that?" asks Sean.

"Well, if we have babies, it all gets complicated, doesn't it?"

"Do you feel we should be boyfriend and girlfriend if we have sex?" asks Sean.

"No. But would you want to fuck me, for goodness sake? I don't you fucking me!" says Laura.

"I wouldn't mind fucking you, Laura."

"Are you serious? Ugh! It's just that you are always horny because you don't have any girlfriends. I'm happy fucking my boyfriends regularly every week, thank you very much," says Laura.

Sean listens to more music and then removes the headphones.

"You mean you haven't fantasized about fucking me...ever?"

"My best friend, you mean. Never!," says Laura.

"You know that you can stay over, my parents are going to New York this weekend. Let's spend the whole weekend together as lovers. We can order in pizzas and not wear any clothes. Then we fuck. You are on the pill, but I can also wear a rubber to make sure," says Sean, "and it's not like we are in a relationship."

"Oh gross, are you mad, Sean?" grimaces Laura.

"You know my new iPhone that you always use? You can have it after the weekend."

"You mean I have to kiss and fuck you for it, the works?...Yuck! But you're on," Laura laughs.

"You mean it? A promise?," asks Sean. "We can watch my parents' porn DVDs because I know where they are."

"Oh really? Sounds fun, actually!" says Laura.

For Sean, that week at university drags on and he longs for Friday night when his parents drive away.

They wait for a big pizza and coke to be delivered and then lock the door and draw all the curtains in their big apartment.

"What now?" Laura asks him standing in

the living room.

"We strip each other slowly," Sean says.

"Everything off?" asks Laura.

"Of course. Let me do you first."

"Gee, I don't know about this now...!" says Laura.

The best friends stand close to each other.

"Kiss me first, like you kiss your boyfriends," commands Sean.

Laura does and gives Sean a lingering wet open-mouth kiss.

"Wow, I've got a hard-on already," says Sean. He kisses her back, more clumsily.

Then he takes his time in lifting Laura's t-shirt to bare her perfect breasts with the softest pink nipples, as she is wearing nothing underneath.

"Oh, Laura!" says Sean as he plows his face into them then sucks each erect nipple in turn.

"Ah, Sean, easy buddy. I'll get too worked up."

"Maybe that's the idea, my sexy stepsister."

Sean opens her tight jeans, pulling them roughly down to reveal a very brief pair of pink knickers that show Laura's fine auburn pubic hair spreading out on either side.

He quickly slides the underwear down and is struck dumb by the sight of Laura's full cunt in front of his face.

"Yes...finally," he mumbles, remembering earlier times when he sneaked views of his Laura dressing and once or twice when she was sleeping over, his own well-kept secret.

The sight of his beautiful and shapely friend naked is sending him wild. He tears off his shirt and quickly pulls down his jeans and undies and kicks them away on the thick carpet.

Laura stands back to marvel at her Sean's formidable cock as it points up at an odd angle, curling up from a thick dark curly bush that hides his little balls.

"Whoa! Not bad either!"

"Let me fuck you now. Or I'll shoot off right here on the carpet!"

"Easy, Sean...The pizza will get cold!"

"Fuck the pizza. I need to fuck you instead, and ASAP!"

Sean pushes his her back onto the big soft lounge. He hurries to open her knees and thighs and shoves his hard dark-pink-headed cock in.

"Aagh, easy Sean!" yells Laura. "Take some time!"

"Sorry, can't wait," says Sean, thrusting wildly now into his Laura's tight hole.

"Oh fuck, oh fuck, Sean," yells Laura. "Where did you get all this energy?"

Head bent and eyes closed, Sean grabs Laura's round hips, to better direct his cock deep inside. Even if he is in a hurry, Sean still lasts a long time, giving his her time to reach her climax long before his does.

"Oh God! Sean!" screams Laura as Sean arches back to discharge his load. He lays in between her long shapely legs as they are spread apart, spent.

The pizza has gone cold on the coffee table.

After their cold supper, the friends' retire to Sean's parents' bedroom where the erotic DVDs were hidden in a separate compartment concealed behind shelves after shelves of movies.

It's clear that presumably his dad is a big collector of erotic DVDs because of the wide range of movies available, from classics and soft porn to ones that shock even from their covers.

They each take a random few then start to play them on the big flat screen, one after the other, and fast forwarding the boring bits.

They make themselves comfortable on his parents' huge bed. Sean props up some pillows in the middle and lays back on them. Then he beckons his sexy friend to sit leaning back between his spread legs.

Laura pulls up her knees and spread her legs wide casually as well for comfort.

The man and woman have never seen anything like those DVDs, they agree. Discounting the obviously fake cries and false orgasmic faces, there are full of genuine scenes that grab them.

Sean realize that they are in his parents' bed like the ones in which they themselves were conceived.

"Let's pretend to be boyfriend and girlfriend," whispers Laura after they turn off the screen, with some relief. "You can be my boyfriend when he takes me to bed. How would we have fucked?"

"Missionary position probably, like this," Laura continues. "I lie on my back and open my legs and you come on top of me."

Not needing a second invitation, Sean stands up and marvels at the sight of her looking at him invitingly and opening her thighs to him. Her pink dramatic gash opens up to reveal a tiny hole that is waiting.

Sean takes his time and gently lies down on her soft body and kisses Laura long and searchingly.

Then he caresses her full and firm breasts, kneading them so that Laura starts to moan.

His hard prick is now stiff and long and is poised on his Laura's pussy.

As his hard penis pushes in, Laura too seems to react as if it was her first fuck. Her eyes close and her lovely pink mouth opens, as if the penis has just breached her virginal hymen, spilling seeping blood.

As Sean moves rhythmically, Laura undulates her body so wonderfully too, as if she is savoring a new-found sexual sensuality.

The two bodies, lost in the huge bed, appear to be able to join all night. And they do for a long time, with the stamina and freshness.

Sean can't really believe what he can see and feel underneath him. His friend's face is stunningly lovely now. Her eyes are closed as she has been transported somewhere else blissful.

Whenever he kisses her soft mouth, and it's often now, and long, she returns his kiss with its searching tongue. Laura is no longer his best friend but has become his loving girlfriend.

Sean can feel that his new girlfriend is close to her orgasm now as her body is striving hungrily, and her cunt is sucking his cock in an overwhelming way.

Her breathing is deeper and her moaning is louder. Sean hangs on hard, waiting for her pleasure.

Strange muttering voices come from her now as she arches her back and pushes up hard her firm body underneath his. He is squeezed hard and fast between her moving thighs.

Sean holds on, as he witnesses the marvelous power of her orgasm as it escalates to a thumping, bed-shaking finish.

Laura holds on tight to him afterward. Her thighs are not letting him move an inch away from her.

She opens her eyes eventually to study him, and it's a different look, changed from the face of the friend that he knows.

"You make a lovely and convincing boyfriend, Sean," she whispers and smiles.

"Thanks," he mumbles.

"Let's be boyfriend and girlfriend again and again and again this weekend, in this bed," she says. "I want much more of it. You have done so well, Sean. I never knew that my best friend could be like this. Can we explore some more of each other? Then I can ditch my boyfriends!" she says, triumphant.

"You can keep your new iPhone, by the way."

CHARA GLADEY

6 SUPER MASSEUR

Lois Lane, blond, full-figured, and fiftyish, has ordered a weekend massage special package from the Super Masseur Company. A black masseur, with a perfect super muscular body, reports to her door, and they spend a weekend like no other in Lois' experience.

To her neighbors, Lois Lane is a sprightly lady, who is out at dawn to exercise. In her pink or yellow tight-fitting track suits that show off her full shapely figure, a few old men breakfasting early sneak a look past their wives sitting opposite to enjoy her regular bustling walks.

Her large full and round bottom, in particular, is quite a sight from behind. Her big bust is nothing to be overlooked either, like two ripe melons bouncing along.

Neighbors suspect that Mrs. Lane is much older than she looks because her husband, who passed away some years ago, was quite an old man with thinning grey hair. But she is still spunky, statuesque with thick light blond hair bouncing behind her.

But the lady keeps every much to herself, and neighbors can greet her only on her exercise walking in the street, or when she rides her bicycle on a sunny day, as no one has been invited to her house. She also declines invitations to their neighborhood parties.

Inside the house, with curtains drawn at night, Lois has a firm rule to always be naked, whatever the weather. She and her late husband had always been house nudists.

Her house is then always well-heated in winter with central heating, open fire and solar panels on the roof for hot water. When snow lies thickly outside, as it does now, the attractive suburban house is a toasty warm retreat from the world.

But Lois has draped her pink flowery dressing gown over the back of the sofa this morning as she is expecting a Super Masseur to call in.

How should she greet him? Au naturel as she usually is, or covered with her pink gown, the concession she makes to the postman? Absolutely nothing on, she decides.

But there he is already, as if swept in by the breeze with specks of snow whirling. She swings the front door wide before the man rings the bell. She didn't hear a car and can't see one parking.

The muscular black man is wearing glasses and has a very handsome face, fairly shining with health. He hides his total surprise very well.

"Well, hi there! I'm Clark," he stammers. "I've come to the right kind of house, I see." He smiles, showing perfect bright teeth.

"This is a no-clothes house," announces Lois. "So would you like to take your clothes off here?"

"Er... sure! Am usually the one requesting that of clients," he says. "Especially sexy and curvaceous ones like yourself!" He grins attractively while easily slipping off his gear.

Lois has to catch her breath and sit down a bit, which she does on her soft lounge. A Black Adonis has come into her house.

There he is with a body as perfect as it comes, a Greek or Roman statue found in art museums that she use to fantasize about and wank to in her bed.

She can certainly masturbate to this ebony god, whose penis is as perfect as she has ever seen one, and she has seen a few variations in her travel, especially after her old hubby passed away, being somewhat of a sex maniac.

The god stands next to her now by the couch, the super dong is hanging directly in front as he massages her on the shoulders with his strong hands.

"At Super Masseur, we offer this weekend package, our best, that you have wisely ordered," he says like a totally convincing salesman.

"This makes me available to you all weekend for as many internal and external massages at any time you wish."

"Ready to have one now?"

"OK," says Lois, still very unsettled by the large, long shiny penis hanging in front of her.

The masseur directs her to lay down on her front on the thick rug in front of the fire. Then he straddles her thick thighs, resting his super cock on her bottom.

Sprinkling fragrant oil on her back, he begins to massage firmly, starting from Lois's neck and shoulders, right down to her full bottom. His marvelous strong fingers rub the fat cheeks then explore the deep valley between them.

Then an oiled thumb slowly slips into her anus then starts to massage inside the tight cavity.

"One of our internal massages," Clark said, smiling.

Lois squirms and wriggles. She is just about to take off to another planet, because his finger feels so good in there. She lets her bum grip the warm finger hard, heightening her own sensation even more.

"Good," he said, "Good."

Now, Clark's steely hands move her thighs apart and begin massaging the inside of them, working their way slowly up to her crotch.

When the comforting fingers reached there, the oiled thumbs are rubbing the full lips of her labia, then again the soft pink valley between them.

Then a thumb finds her large clitoris. Many men have told Lois that her button was bigger than normal.

"Wow!," he says simply.

His massaging of her vital large spot is sending Lois balmy. Despite herself, she is shaking and gyrating on the rug out of control.

"Now another internal massage," says Clark.

Lois feels his huge cock firmly pushing its way into her cunt.

"Woah, I don't think it will fit!," she says.

"Don't worry, relax."

It does fit somehow and begins to slide in and out smoothly.

"Oh, my God, my God," moans Lois. In all her years of fucking, she has never felt anything like this. The movement of the man, now nicely heavy on top of her, is firm and regular, as if his piston can pump away all weekend.

But Lois knows that she was not going last another minute like this, and lunges forward, arching her back to scream the way she has never screamed before when fucking.

"Oh, stop please, stop! I need a breather after that," she says.

Clark slips off from the top of her as suddenly as if he has just levitated. One minute his weight was there, the next it wasn't.

"Oh wow. I'm going to be dead after a couple of days of this, I'm sure," she says.

Lois has turned over now, spreading

apart her legs and thighs to let sweat dry.

"You have a lovely full womanly body," says the marvel of a man as he lies beside her.

"So men tell me. I keep it well exercised everyday also," Lois says.

"But you didn't come!," she says.

"Oh, I'm a Super Masseur, you see, and I can control when, and if, I should ejaculate," says Clark. "It's part of our training, if you like.

"Shall we, to the Jacuzzi to wash off your sweat?," he asks.

"Sure, it's upstairs in the bedroom," she says.

Before she knows it, Super Masseur has sprung in a flash to his feet, and she is already lifted and laying across his arms.

"How did you do that? I know, Super Masseur," she says, laughing.

The man fairly skips up her stair, as if her body is as light as a little doll that she is definitely not.

The warm, bubbling Jacuzzi is heavenly, especially with this hunk of a man sitting between her spread out legs, with her feet surfacing either side of his broad shoulders. She leans back and thinks why she should deserve this.

Lois feels bold enough now to reach under the water to feel Clark's dong. She has never felt anything like this member that is round and tough as rubber. She feels the formidable bulb at the end of it and the little vertical lip at the end of it that her fingers can open and play with.

She slides her open vagina up to the hard police baton and positions the prick on her big clitoris. The sensation knocks her backwards, as if some electricity has passed from the penis to her.

Moving her vagina up and down and using the cock as a big dildo, Lois very soon brings herself to another jerking finish that sends ripple-like tsunamis around the tub.

"Oh shit, what was that?" she moans.

"At your service, ma'am," says the man with a wide smile. "You may be ready now for our third type of internal massage."

The black Adonis now kneels up between her thighs, and his might ebony missile is pointing threateningly at her face.

"Good God!," she says before the hard instrument is trying part her fleshy lips.

Lois opens her mouth wide, and savors the warm cock slipping in, filling the full cavity of her mouth.

It moves gently in and out of her mouth, feeling excruciatingly good somehow. She sucks it now hard like an oversized lollipop, enjoying herself.

"Do you want me to finish inside your mouth?," says the man, still moving gently with no apparent urgency."

Lois nods her head, as she can't do anything else.

And presto on call, as if the tap is turned on, hot semen fills her mouth and runs down her throat. Lois has to swallow carefully for fear of choking.

But it doesn't choke her, but instead, fills

her mouth and stomach with a kind of revitalizing power.

"Wow," says Lois as she helps Clark wash his penis that is still erect and hard, in the bath water.

"Did you come? I didn't hear you," she asks.

"Yes, obviously!" he says, pointing to the sperm-coated penis that is being washed.

The fourth internal massage comes later that night at the end of her big bed when the Super Masseur has her resting on her front there and penetrates her from behind.

As with all the fucks with this man, it was a new, a phenomenal, and a very memorable experience.

And this weekend, Lois is fucking everywhere, on the stairs, in the kitchen, and in the shower again. The remarkable God is virile is never tired or flaccid.

Sharing her bed with this man is comforting and even loving. She has booked him to return again the next weekend without fail.

A rather puzzling thing happened though on Monday morning when Lois is expecting to say goodbye to her Super Masseur at the front door.

When she wakes and stretches after a torrid night, her vagina is nicely burning, and her thighs complaining as if they had run a marathon during the night, which they did.

Her bedroom window was ajar, letting the snowy air in, and Clark is no longer to be found in the house.

7 GOOD NEIGHBOR FLO

Florence sees herself as a nurse of some sort. All her short life, she has always been moved by loneliness and suffering in this world as witness only in this inner Chicago city neighborhood of hers where she grew up.

She realized how lonely were the Billys, Patricks and Dougies of this world whom she used to greet on her way back to and from school.

They were sitting on their front porch or on their doorsteps with their mangy pets when she left to catch the school bus, and they were still there when she returned home.

Not to mention the hobos in the park and many alley ways, and the also the destitute women around as well who were as lonely and vulnerable.

So, it's not for nothing that her mother

named her after Florence Nightingale.

So after a year or two at university, majoring in sociology, Flo came up with her own neighborhood scheme that that she is proud of, but that no one knows anything about, except the grateful recipients, who have come to look forward to it and relying on it.

Being Friday night, Flo is free from her busy work life. As usual, she first runs a bath to soak her limbs and get ready.

Then, she dressed in her casual bright short dress, she skips out into the warm summer night and jumps on to her bicycle to ride to her work.

Billy is her first patient always, as he lives nearest her student apartment. His grimy door is ajar, as he knows that Flo comes every Friday at this time.

"Knock, knock. Hey, Billy," she yells into the dark and stuffy bed-sit. No reply. He has probably dozed off, but hopefully not died on her.

As usual, Flo picks up very smelly socks from the littered floor, which she holds at arm's length with her other fingers clamped on her nose. Old, dirty underwear has to be put in a laundry pile as well.

As she runs water in the sink over plates caked with grimy gravy leftover from who knows when, a thick hand has come around from the back to grab hard and deep at her crotch.

"Jeez, Billy! You scared me," Flo yells.

"Sorry, love. Didn't mean to do that," says a gruff and shaky voice. "Just couldn't resist it when I see you bending over the sink in this sexy short skirt of yours."

"How are you, man?" Flo asks. Billy is dressed in relatively clean striped pajamas.

"I was just in the bath, getting ready for you," says the old man, whose long untidy grey hair badly needs cutting.

"That's nice, Billy," she says, roughing his hair. "I'll cut that next time."

"Whoah! What do we have here?" says Flo.

Billy's bony prick is pointing straight out of the fly opening in his pajamas.

"I need to fuck you quickly, my angel," says the old man, grabbing hard the cheeks of her bum and pushing her against the kitchen sink. "I'm as horny as a coot."

"Didn't know that coots were horny. But I know you always are, Billy Goat - and at your age too!"

"Can't help it, Dearie, if I am virile," says Billy shakily, as Flo detaches a condom packet from a string of them in her handbag.

"You are that for sure, Billy," she says as she expertly slips the condom on the long penis.

"Oh, fuck!," screams Flo, as Billy's long hard bone has quickly sneaked past her undies and right up her vagina.

"Whoah, take your time, Billy. Enjoy it!"

"I am enjoying it, girlie, but I got to come now!" croaks Billy, his strong bony body butting hard against the welcoming harbor of Flo's open kindly thighs. Soon he is shuddering and spluttering all over her uncontrollably.

Flo gets worked up too, and it feels very sexy to be fucked standing up in the kitchen like that.

"My God, girlie. You are so good to me."

Flo's second patient of her nightly neighborhood nursing round, as she likes to see it, is sitting on the steps at the door of his lodging building. The large fat Irishman has a hard life having to look after his sickly fat wife every day of the week.

"Come inside a bit and I'll give you a massage," says Flo. "Hot night, eh?"

Nurse Flo usually tends to this patient here on the stairs the corridor that go up to other floor in front of Patrick's ground floor lodging. She never goes into the apartment to disturb his wife.

As usual too, Flo sit a while with her obese man, smelling his sweat, and chats to him about the condition of his wife and how his day was. She has been able to help him at times to take his wife to some different clinics for her various medical conditions.

As he sits on the stairs, Patrick likes Flo to stand between his fat legs spread apart. He cuddles her tightly, and rests his bald head on her breasts, as if to take refuge there from the burden of his week.

Tonight, his thick hands are as usual groping around Flo's full and round bottom, with his fingers under her flimsy briefs and cupped around her soft cheeks and into the deep cleft between them.

"Oh, you feel so good, love," he says with his eyes shut. Then he pulls her underwear to her angles.

The front door of the building opens, and the tall black Joey stumbles in.

"Howdy, Pat and Flo," he says, as he squeezes past them on the narrow stairs to go up to his room. "Hot night, guys."

Patrick has easily lifted Flo now so that her lithe legs are spread awkwardly on either side of his round belly while her bare feet try to balance on the steps.

Her full cunt, with its soft blond hair, is spread open in front of Pat's face. Flo shudders now as the man, not-too-gently, presses his big nose into it.

Again, the man's large head and face rest there, having found a haven from all the trials of the previous weeks, since she last called in.

Flo squirms now as Patrick's thick lips and warm tongue part and licks her most sensitive groove, now open to his service.

In this way too, of course, Nurse Flo gets her full reward. Patrick knows what he can do with that tongue of his and he is relentless until he can sense that his angelic nurse is also getting off herself.

Flo has to hold on to his head now, pressing her clitoris even harder into the man's lips. When the sensitive and hard knob slips onto his big nose, Flo is at the end of her tethers, her angelic face grimacing to the sky.

"You are something, Nurse Flo," says Patrick.

Some nights, Flo likes to manipulate Patrick's prick, rolling a condom on to it, handling and stroking it and have fun sucking it until it throbs to shoot off.

But tonight she is late and has to move to another patient.

It's not easy to find the hobo Doug, especially at night.

He lives in the park but moves around to stop the cops pestering him too much. To be fair, the police don't do anything to him, as they know that he refuses to go to any of the city's homes.

He is at one of his overnight spots tonight deep in the shrubbery to one side of the park away from pathways.

Flo parks her cycle near an elm and walks in with her little torch shining.

"Hey, Doug. How are you?" she calls out into the darkness. A rustling of surprise in the bush.

"Good, Sis Flo. Ah had a good week," says Doug.

The lanky Black man was lying on a big bed of newspapers in the middle of the grove.

"Have you been eating well, Dougie?"

"Can't complain, and the cops have left me alone."

"But shush ... I think there are a couple of lovers in the other bush near the lake. Don't want them to come to bother us."

Flo goes over to sit astride the man's hip on top of his bulging genital mound.

"What will it be? The usual, Dougie?"

"Oh yes please, Sis," he says.

"Get up then, and I'll wait here for you. Here take this," Flo says and tears off another condom.

"Aw, do I have to use that damn thing?"

"Yes, Dougie! We don't know where you've been, do we?," says Flo, smiling.

Doug likes to slip off his grimy trousers, but still keeps his dirty big boots on to fuck. He stands up in the dark to do this, hanging his smelly pants neatly on a convenient branch.

In the gloom he looks like some kind of specter wandered in from Halloween night.

His grey and black hair is curly and long, framing a bony face with two white round eyes, his wiry body is long and thin like a skeleton, and there is rancid smell floating from him in the warm night air.

The Grim Reaper also carries a long erect lethal weapon between his legs that is now pointing directly at Flo lying on the newspapers on the ground.

As it's a warm night, Flo has stripped off everything of hers. As the Reaper shuffles forward, she opens her thighs wide.

"Come to your angel," she says.

"Oh, my God," cries Doug, as he swiftly falls on her.

Above the noises of Dougie and the newspapers crumbling, Flo hears distinct giggling coming from the dark bushes and glimpses the naked figures of two Black lovers, enjoying the scene.

8 SPRING VIRGINS

It's springtime at last in the prairie after a particularly long and hard winter. White patches of snow, soiled now, can still be found in the hollows in the ground, under bushes and next to the gnarled trees in the forest.

Pale purple and pink crocuses and dainty white snowdrops are pushing through the grey dead grasses that have been buried for months under the thick snow and are only now touched by the sun for the first time this year.

Two brunette women who are identical twins and both university students of visual arts have been relishing a chance of their lifetime.

They had both been invited to come to spend the long winter with legendary artist Henry Wyeth to learn from him and to be his models at his studio farm in the middle of nowhere in Maine.

They have never asked why the artist chose them, but they guessed that he wanted models who were mirror images of each other for effects. He was probably also drawn to the rustic Germanic beauty: all pale-skinned and strong-limbed.

The handsome and rugged Wyeth, as craggy as the rocky outcrops on his spreading farm, has been a perfect teacher and a gentleman, who unfortunately did not lay a hand on them during the long dark days when they were working long hours in his barn, which was heated by a roaring wood burner.

It was lucky for the women that the barn was always warm because they were both always modeling for the master painter totally in the nude.

If the truth be known, both women were still pure virgins.

Their strict Calvinist parents had tried to instill in them the joy of purity and the satisfaction of keeping their precious hymens intact for their wedding nights as valuable dowries for their husbands.

When Henry first asked them to pose in the nude, the girls blushed deeply and did not know how to answer the master. They finally agreed and, from the very first session, very much enjoyed the overwhelming erotic sensation of being bare in front of a man for the very first time in their lives.

They posed in innocent semblance, mostly singly and sometimes together, such as standing and gazing at the artist or lying on the hay to show the devastating beauty of their delectable round asses.

With the snowstorms howling outside, the women confided in each other that they often wished the very attractive painter would have tumbled them into his bed, either singly or both at once.

To lose their virginity to this talented man would be a good way to thumb their noses at their Spartan Midwest religious upbringing.

But the artist, while obviously appreciating placing the beauty of their attractive bodies large on big canvases, unfortunately never took liberties with them.

But the girls are staying longer with him so they still hold on to their collective hopes that he might want to get physical.

In the meantime, as they did secretly behind the locked door in their shared bedroom in the attic back home, the nubile twins now cuddle in one bed together, their limbs and long straight brunette hair entwined, creating their own beautiful Gemini star sign.

They each had their own vibrator to masturbate to simulate their sexual desires. They would whisper what each wanted the Master to do to them - each with their own sexual desires as the vibrator guided them to their own individual climaxes. They would allow their hands and fingers explore their clits and other parts of their own bodies—careful not to touch each other. Though they were twins and know each other so well, they had the desire to share a man, but never to explore each other's bodies.

Invariably though, their index or middle fingers find their way "home" to the comforting warm and moist holes of their own vaginas to rest on and reassuringly caress their virginal hymens.

They both move their vibrators faster and harder at their own control Then comes the well-practiced tracing of the fingers on their softest paths slightly north to the clitoris mounds that are now erect.

The fingers take their own sweet time to gently knead and circle these magical spots, until the women hit their marks usually always spot-on together, gripping on to each of their vibrators more tightly, calling out in climax.

Lotte and Ulrike are able to see themselves even more clearly now, interpreted through the eyes of the master painter, who has simply laid them bare for the world to see, as large as life on the big oil canvases.

They can see the unique mixture of their own youthful emptiness and innate psychological depth seen through their painted eyes that look out from their portraits.

The women are also struck by their own beauty that moves viewers of the paintings with its sheer erotic power.

But over the winter, the women have

decided to give their virginity to someone other than their future husbands. As it doesn't look like that someone will be the famous Henry, the women have chosen Andrew, the lanky blond and shy young man from the neighboring farm.

The blond farm hand, whose parents are Swedish immigrants, has been coming around to help Henry with farm chores, such as the constant chopping of firewood in the snow and breaking the ice in the well to draw up water in a bucket.

The women have come to like him, as for them it looks as if he has grown straight out of this beautiful and severe natural landscape that they love.

But how are they going to persuade him? The twins decide that it's best just to go for it.

So after his usual day of farm work at the house, the women each link one arm with his on either side of him and pull him through the garden of the old apple trees, where delicate little white and pink flowers are budding, to take the shy boy on a walk.

Andrew protests meekly that he is expected home soon for dinner, but to deaf ears. The young women lead the poor man now into the cool forest where a new universe of soft green leaves is budding on every branch.

In their own wanderings, Lotte and Ulrike have found a lovely pine needle-filled hollow in a little forest clearing that has a patch of blue sky above it. Little wild flowers grow in this hushed place where the virgins would very soon offer their virginity to nature.

If Andrew doesn't have other ideas, that is.

Wearing their favorite identical short white dresses with delicate blue flower patterns, the sisters sit Andrew on a fallen trunk in the clearing and themselves on the ground on either side of him.

"Can you do us a big favor, Andrew?" asks Lotte finally.

"Yes, what is it?" asks the young man.

"Fuck us," says Ulrike.

Andrew is wide-eyed. The women laugh.

"You see, we want to lose our virginity. So can you help us?" asks Lotte.

"You are the first women that I know, and I don't know what to do."

"So you are a virgin too!" says Ulrike. "The gods are lucky then. Three virgins to be sacrificed! Let's teach each other."

Before he decides to change his mind, not that his mind is made up actually, the twins help him get up.

"The first thing to do is for all of us to get undressed," says Lotte, who starts now to take off the sweaty clothes from the poor man.

The twins hold their breaths at the sight of the golden muscular body standing naked like a skittish colt. They quickly drop their flimsy dresses and underpants, and the three perfect bodies now stand simply naked like figures in an Italian Renaissance painting.

Lotte holds up two twigs now for Ulrike to pick.

"Let Andrew pick," says Ulrike. "The short one is me."

Red-faced, the young man duly does as he is told while his left hand is vaguely trying to shield his long cock, which is insisting on curving up erect in the presence of naked females.

His fingers hold up a short twig.

The twins look at each other, smile and give each other the look of excitement that their nights of sexual wishes is about to happen..

Ulrike lays down on the soft old pine needles and spreads her legs. Lotte leads Andrew by the arm to show him how to kneel between her twin sister's legs.

With her hand trembling, Lotte holds the man's now visibly hard cock, now the size of a branch, and positions its brute helmeted head on her sister's small pink opening.

"Slowly now, or it will hurt her," she says as she gently pushes in Andrew's perfect muscular backside.

Ulrike struggles now and her hand closes on the pine needles on the ground.

"Ah, Lotte, ah. Now!" she moans as the colt's long penis spears more than half of its length in. "Ah. It's done!"

Lotte retreats to sit nearby to watch as Andrew' cock pushes in and draws out between her sweet sister's thighs. There is virginal blood showing on the shaft.

The man is rather merciless now, his strong body pressing on her gentle sister, as he quickly ejaculates long and hard, his beautiful upper body arching back, then flopping hard on the soft small breasts of the sacrificed virgin.

He rolls off now to lay spent on the needles beside a beaming Ulrike.

For Lotte's turn, the twins reverse roles, with Ulrike lying by Lotte's side and holding her hand at the point when a man's cock makes the breach.

As the tireless farm hand makes his charge and Ulrike bucks to her peak at the same time, the sisters smile at each other, finally on their journey as women of the world.

9 JEN'S DINER

Jen's Diner, or the name should really read Jen and Wendy's Diner, is not right on the busy interstate highway through Arkansas. But motorists and truck drivers taking the freeway exit towards the little town of Little Rock, soon come to it, shining like a chromed cigar or penis.

Fat Jen and her long-time bed and business partner, Wendy, have bought this franchise from a chain based in California that has these retro sixties' oblong metal tubes, looking really like garish penises rolled off by the road side.

Diners can select bopping, swinging, and syrupy pop music from jukebox selectors on their tables of the in the cool retro interior that is stylish and tastefully colorful, putting one right into an interior design page of a faded magazine from the nostalgic sixties.

Plump Jen and thin bespectacled Wendy

live in a little house set back among the trees around the back for some very prosperous years now.

But for their good money, the two lesbians have to work long hours until 2 am every night of the week. They have help from sexy Charlene, a local Little Rock young single mother, whose full figure bursts out of her tight-fitting pink uniform with its miniskirt struggling to conceal her polka-dotted undies, when she wears some, that is.

While being known as a lesbian couple, Jen and Wen are partial to the he-men and he-women, drivers, and salesmen, whose cars, trucks, and delivery vans fill up their parking lot much of the time.

Jen and Wen have never had to advertise their diner. Somehow word of mouth gets around and business is always good, when their menu have the usual fare of burgers, steak, coffee, and fries, and nothing out of the ordinary. All very well cooked, mind you.

But actually, it's not quite true that there is nothing out of the ordinary.

The first thing that even the most unobservant and short-sighted diners notice, often to their utter surprise, is that the three attractive women staff sometimes don't wear any underwear under their form-fitting short miniskirts as they work.

The women would like to go bare down there all the time, but sometimes are forced to put on some protection if there happen to be diners who may get offended or cause trouble for the restaurants, such as clergymen, young families, countrywomen association members, or the cops themselves.

The second innovation, equally successful, is a cryptic little symbol appearing after the list of ice creams and desserts on the menu: a line drawing that looks like a hairy coffee bean. The description says, "After-dinner house special," with the price of $50, and customers can order it as such or by just pointing to the spot on the menu without saying anything.

Tonight, for instance, it's a little quiet after the evening meal rush. Some truckies are tucking into their steaks, cooked expertly by Wen in the kitchen. Big Jen waddles nicely to a new guy, middle-aged with spectacles, who looks like an insurance salesman.

"How are you, Bud?" Jen greets him in her usual casual way.

"Good, thanks. Nice diner, you got," says the man.

"Why, thank you kindly. We're proud of it," says Jen. "What will it be?"

As the little man orders, Jen lifts up her left foot with its high-heeled shoe to rest casually on the bench on the other side of the table.

The move exposes her bulging fat cunt falling out from under her tight pink uniform miniskirt, looking very much like the hairy coffee bean symbol on the menu.

Jen loves to see the new customers' faces when they glimpse these suddenly exposing vulvas. Their surprise is total. Most people look back to the menu and pretend that they hadn't seen anything at all.

Likewise does the insurance man, who glances back at the menu after being hit almost physically by the sight of Jen's cunt.

"That's this," says Jen, pointing to the after-dinner special. "Good value, if I say so myself," says Jen with a wink and a friendly smile. "Helps you on your journey very well."

"Oh no, thank you," mumbled the embarrassed man. "I'm a happily married man, thank you."

"I understand, Bud. Many of those come through this place," says Jen, wisely. "So, just the cheeseburger, Budweiser, and coffee?"

"Yes, please."

As Jen is picking up the man's plates and coffee cup after he had a good meal, she barely heard the shy guy say, "Could I change my mind and try the special?"

"Sure thing," says Jen gently. "You won't regret it, Bud. Follow me."

Jen makes sure that either Wen or Charlene sees her leading the customer to the back door.

Outside there is a green mowed area under the kitchen window.

"We provide the $50 quickies here, Bud, standing up usually," Jen says, her arm around the little man's shoulder already as soon as they are outside. "Do you want it in front or in the back?"

"Er... the front," mumbles the man.

Fat Jen expertly pulls the man's trousers

down around his ankles and leans back against the corrugated shiny metal surface of the diner, hitches up her skirt a little to expose the big mother-earth bulge of her tummy and her full Venus mound, and opens her large thighs to reveal a wide-open hairy vulva.

"Hail Mary, Mother of God!" says the little man, as he crosses himself and aims his small prick right into be fully swallowed up by hot flesh.

The little man is working hard now. It may have been awhile since he is having his particular pleasure and he is making the most of it.

Jen catches sight of her lover Wen looking on, as she often does from the kitchen window where she has a box-seat view. They exchange a knowing smile, and Jen can see that Wen is also amused by the earnestness of the little traveler.

The man gives a couple of more little shoves, then buries his face, glasses and all, right into the deep valley between Jen's breasts to finish up.

As the pleased little man leaves to go to his small car, the night becomes filled with vibrating rumbling as a big motorcycle gang converges on the lonely diner from all directions.

"Oh, my Lord!" yells Charlene and the women rush to change into emergency longer skirts and slip on their undies underneath. As the first of the riders stomp in noisily, the ladies have replaced most of the menus on the tables with emergency ones that don't show the hairy coffee beans.

Soon the whole place is all filled with large black-leather-clad male members of the Coffin Cheaters, some showing scary pictures of skeletons on their backs.

The women quickly confer in the kitchen but they know the procedure that they have practiced. Wen has an emergency number of the local police patrol car writ large near the phone. There is also a licensed loaded pistol in a drawer in the kitchen.

The ladies would normally humor the dangerous guys and take no chance by crossing any of them.

Whole lot of beers and burgers are being ordered, and Wen is flat out cooking them.

From the corner of her eyes, Jen sees one of the burly guys at a table of three pointing at the menu and asking Charlene something about it. Then they all joke and laugh. Luckily, men at nearby tables do not join in.

"Shit!" Jen says to herself, an old menu wasn't collected.

"The three guys have ordered the house special," reports grim-faced Charlene when she comes to the counter with her orders. "I told them OK, but one at a time. I couldn't tell them 'no,' as a biker friend of theirs has recommended it."

"Take care, Doll," says Jen. "Don't allow any rough stuff."

"I'll try," says Charlene.

After their supper, many of the riders are fortunately roaring off on their Harley's.

Charlene now leads a hulking, black-bearded man with a huge beer gut to the back door. As Wen watches the diner, to make sure that none of the men makes a move to the back door as well, Jen peers out of the kitchen window down on to the lawn below.

The monster of a man burps loudly, quickly unbuckles his huge leather belt, and unzips to free a large meaty truncheon that aims straight out. He roughly bends Charlene over, flicking her skirt over her back, then bludgeons right in between her legs and large round bum.

Jen sees Charlene's face grimacing then a look of alarm comes over the face as the two other large riders come out through the back door.

Jen's hand has reached into the drawer and touches the pistol. She has never shot anyone but would not hesitate to do so now, having taken some training.

One man with a huge torso has stepped in front of Charlene, so that her head now pushes against his bulging mass.

His large hands are roughly pushing under Charlene's blouse to free her melon-shaped breasts so that they hang down and swing as her body continues to be rammed from behind.

Not yet, thinks Jen, not yet.

Both the new arrivals are now baring their sizeable penises that they are stoking in readiness for their turn, for which they fortunately seem to be prepared to wait.

Amid all that, Jen can see Charlene's face looking back. She is nodding with a slight smile. Jen relaxes her grip on the gun.

It has been a busy night at the retro roadside diner.

10 FINDING THEIR LOLITA

Professor Sevastian Noskov, the grandson of master writer Vadik Noskov, comes to America from Russia to look for his grandfather's Lolita. Soon, he finds her, young and auburn-haired, in an autumnal village in New Hampshire. But Lolita's mother has a surprise for them both.

The old car looks as if it has just driven out of the forest road straight out of a time maybe 50 years ago. It's driving strangely too, meandering, as if the driver can't steer all that well.

Dr. Sevastian Noskov is well aware of the similarity between this reality and the scene from the latest Lolita movie when Jeremy Irons was driving this way. Having seen this favorite movie many, many, many times, Sevastian is surprised to discover real versions of the scenes everyday now in this wonderful part of America, turning into a brilliant show of autumnal colors.

Like his granddad and masterful author Vadik Noskov, Dr. Sevastian teaches literature but back home in Russia. His PhD thesis was on Lolita, his granddad's masterpiece that has inspired this sensitive grandson all his young life.

Now he has a once-in-a-lifetime chance to find his own Lolita in the America that Vadik had loved.

Using his rare sabbatical time and all his savings, Professor Sevastian plans to spend the month that he has available simply to follow the wanderings of Humbert, the main character in the book.

Sevastian firmly believes in serendipity. If he is meant to find this young flower of an all-American girl to give his heart to on a plate, he will on this trip. This old car that he has bought will enable him to do that.

He didn't at first notice the name of this New Hampshire village, so glorious at the moment that he was cruising on this cool sparkling morning. The beauty of its tree-lined streets and houses, carpeted by hues of fallen leaves, slows his old car.

On the lawn under a big glorious tree, a young girl reads a book while on a swing in the ray of autumn sunshine.

Even from this far, her youthful beauty is arresting. Her wavy auburn hair catches the sun and blends in with the prevailing autumnal colors of the day. She must have been a stunning nymphet some years earlier.

Sevastian brakes softly and pulls over

some way from the house. He uses a small pair of binoculars to study her, as he has many times on his American Lolita search so far.

The beauty of nymphets that he has seen, and photographed with his camera with its little telephoto lens, would fill a good-size album back home.

The nymphets in Russia are of course equally spectacular, if not more so with their blond, lanky, nubile beauty. But he is looking for his grandfather's American Lolita.

He may not even take a photo of this girl on her swing. She is too old, looking at least 18 or 19. The flower bud has bloomed, but still gloriously so.

The American beauty drops her book on the lawn and begins to swing from a thick branch of an oak. Through the binocular, he sees clearly that the naughty older nymphet is actually still wearing her nightie, white with tiny pink vagina rosettes on it.

She kicks her perfect long legs now, spreading them apart at the top of her swing, to reveal to the binoculars the soft brown fuzzy bush of her young cunt, as the definitely naughty girl is wearing no underwear.

Dr. Sevastian can't put down his binoculars. Too old she may be to be a nymphet, but the search for his American Lolita is ending here.

His nubile beauty skips off the swing; bends down to pick up her book, offering the binoculars another flash of her pert young bum; and disappears into the house.

There is a little handwritten notice near the front door through the porch that conveniently says: "Boarder wanted."

Sevastian sits waiting in the car as morning suburban life comes to the pretty street. He then put on his jacket and a hat and walks to the front of the attractive two-story house and rings the bell.

His spectacular Lolita answers the door. She is dressed in tight jeans and a blouse now.

"Hi," she says with a smile.

"Hello," says Sevastian. "I would like a room."

The girl hesitates, with a startled look.

"Mum," she yells upstairs. "Someone wants a room." She smiles at him again and seems to study him. Sevastian meets her eyes and he melts a little. She then smiles a very cryptic smile.

Sevastian finds Mrs. Jane Robinson, as that is what Lolita's mum's name is, quite an attractive vivacious and, as his American novels tell him, "spunky" woman. They "hit it off at first sight," as books also say.

"Of course, we have room for a learned gentleman like you," says Jane and took him to a cozy small room downstairs at the back with a big study desk that looks out to the garden.

As they try to squeeze past each other behind the desk, Jane's vulva mound swelling out from her woolen tight-fitting dress brushes the bulge of her new tenant's penis hill as the bodies are jammed behind the study chair.

"Oh, my," says Jane, only slightly flustered. "I was going to charge you $150 a week, but it looks very much like $100 will be enough, my dear Russian man!"

Her strong hand has pushed straight into the top of Sevastian's trousers and grabbed the Sputnik rocket standing up hard and ready to launch.

Sevastian fumbles also and holds on awkwardly to Jane's breasts that are also push hard against his palms.

"Oh, Lordy," Jane says. "Are all Russian folks such fast workers?"

"Never fucked a Communist before, but here goes...," she says. "Don't worry, Dominique is off to her classes now so we have the house to ourselves."

"We are not all Communists, by the way," says Sevastian, laughing.

Mrs. Robinson has bent over and put her hands on the bed and pushed out her large shapely bottom, moving her thighs apart.

Sevastian doesn't wait for further invitation but flips Jane's dress on to her back and pull her brief purple panties down to her knees. He then drops his own gear to reveal the Sputnik rocket that is poised for entry back to earth.

That's the rather shocking image that confronts Dominique, seen through the side bedroom's glass window, as the daughter sneakily doubles back around to the back garden to see what her mum is up to.

She has never seen her mum's cunt before and marvels how large, open, and hairy it is. Scary, really, compared to her own little tight one.

Then she thinks that her mum may have caught a glimpse of her even when Jane's contorted face is shaking from the regular shoving of the moaning Sevastian behind her. Dominique runs back and heads for her bus, being a bit late.

The new family of three was quiet at first during their first dinner together that evening. Jane has cooked a tasty beef Stroganoff for her tenant, the only food she knows that may be from Sevastian's country.

Sitting opposite her darling tenant now, she opens her knees under the plastic tablecloth and squeezes Sevastian's legs with them playfully.

Amazingly it's Dominique who starts to speak about the book that she is studying for creative writing at university – Vadik Noskov's Lolita.

When she hears that Sevastian is Russian foremost expert on that very book, she practically jumps on his lap. She is more astounded to be told that Sevastian is even Noskov's grandson.

Mrs. Robinson beams with happiness to see her daughter getting on so well already with her lodger, upon whom she is hatching a secret design.

"Come to my study after dinner tonight and I can help you with the assignment that you have to hand in soon," says Sevastian, neatly seizing his chance.

His Lolita jumps up and plants a wet kiss

on his cheek.

The professor has changed into his pajamas and is pacing the room, nervous, when he heard a soft knock at the door. His Lolita has only a short nightie on.

She flies into his arms right away and hugs him.

"Am I your Lolita, Humbert?" she asks. "I couldn't believe it when I saw you. You stepped out of the book I was reading."

"Well, yes, Lolita. I came to America to look for you and I have found you," says Sevastian. "And I won't let you go." He means that.

They kiss long and hard. "Do what you want with me, Humbert. Fuck me!"

With trembling hands, he removes Dominique's flimsy clothes to reveal a perfect Lolita that he had seen again and again previously in his mind.

He kneels to kiss her bush of soft auburn pubic hair and can stay there forever. He carries his Lolita over to his bed, like a bride on her wedding night.

Dominique waits as Sevastian undresses completely and then parts her legs and climbs on top of her.

The young Noskov gently enters his Lolita, as if carefully breaching her virginity. He feels her tightness around his penis and her softness everywhere else. The fictional lovebirds are just working up to their first orgasm together.

"Is this a private party or can anyone join in?" comes Jane's loud voice. She is standing at the door, staring down on the bed. But she is naked as well.

Then she smiles widely. "You guys have your blast first, then come up to my bedroom where the bed has room for three fucking lovers."

After a torrid night, the likes of which Professor Nobokov has never dreamed of in his Moscow study, Mrs. Robinson springs her surprise.

With the delectable Lolita asleep, worn out, showing her lovely bum, Jane straddles Sevastian and whispers.

"Marry me today, and we'll come to live with you in Russia. You can fuck me and your Lolita forever then.

"But I'll be extra careful not to be conveniently run over by a car as I am in the lovely book that incidentally is my favorite also," she says with an endearing and knowing smile.

11 MARY'S ADULT DOLLS

Mary Pinocchio makes dolls, very special adult ones.

She comes from a family of dollmakers that can be traced back in family history books to a certain Alberto Pinocchio in the last century, who made wooden puppets and other toys in the Tyrolean village high up in the Austrian Alps.

An enduring local legend has it that Alberto made one puppet, dressed like an Austrian mountain boy, which came alive during the night of the full moon and danced about all by itself on the shelf among the other wooden toys.

The legend is much-loved by children. It is the subject of countless children's storybooks read at night in bed to wide-eyed youngsters; its popularity was only increased by the production and release of an animated film.

Mary knows that the family legend is true.

She has lived in the black forested hills around the town of Salem, Massachusetts, with its unfortunate grim history of witch hunts in the seventeenth century, for as long as she can remember. Given the area's history, she likes to encourage the town folk's suspicion that she is an original witch herself.

She lives in an isolated log house in the forest, high up in the mountains. She prefers to dress in bright clothing while at home; in the summer, she often wears no clothes at all.

But on her infrequent trips into the town of Salem, the "witch" dresses all in black, to match her full head of jet-black hair. She carries a black walking stick, even though she doesn't need it for walking.

It's all good for business.

And business has been really picking up since she got hooked up with the Internet, something that she has resisted for a long time. Now she has a long waiting list for her "fucking dolls." Most of her customers are happy to wait patiently for their turn.

Fucking dolls? That's how they have come to be known, for better or worse. They are, in fact, magical toys that are anatomically correct and made with adult entertainment in mind.

To say "made" is not quite correct either. Mary's dearest mother, Heidi, taught her only daughter how to stuff the foot-long dolls with cotton and make their bodies out of pieces of cotton cloth sewn together.

The dolls are of both sexes and come in a variety of shapes and are modeled from real people around the district who are game enough to come to sit and model naked for Mary.

It would be quicker to photograph these local models, but Mary prefers to make 12-inch tall little sculptures out of clay while the models pose.

Mary also uses herself and her late husband as models.

Mother and daughter then spend their day, often working well into the night, sewing the dolls' limbs and embroidering each hair onto their bodies—thick hair on their heads, shorter eyebrows and facial hair, and curly hairs above their groin.

The end products are small versions of the townspeople of Salem, all lying about naked, piled up on Mary's work table. The ladies also make clothes for the lifelike dolls, which are sold separately so that owners can dress or undress their adult dolls at will.

But the doll-makers' meticulous work is completed only on the nights of the full moon.

Mary has never forgotten the first time that her mother propped against a pillow on her bed two dressed dolls of a fat man and a blond young woman, both recognizable as residents of the town.

While Mary watched from the other end of the bed, the patch of moonlight slowly moved over the seated and clothed figures.

The dolls then began to move of their own accord!

They stood up, kissed and cuddled each other. The foot-tall lovers then began to help each other undress.

Mary saw a tiny penis grow and point up as the blond woman squatted down with her realistic thighs open. The tiny woman put the dick in her mouth and performed a long realistic fellatio bathed in moonlight, much to the appreciation of her little man.

Then the little man mounted her and the little lovers fucked away, lost in the middle of the big bed. Mary saw them both having a wild orgasm, without any noise as the dolls are mute, then later separate from each other and flopped backward, spread out on the bed all worn out.

Heidi left the dolls where they were and she and Mary left the room. Heidi told her daughter that after their realistic rest, the fucking dolls would start again and keep going until sunrise.

That night, Mary didn't dare go into the room where all the other dolls were stored; her mother warned her that, whether moonlight strikes on them or not, the soft toys become fully active and mobile when the full moon shines.

In a small house in a boring suburb of Miami, where she has lived all her life,

Gertrude has waited impatiently for the night of the full moon.

As usual, in the tropical night, the sensual lady closes all her blinds and relishes the pleasure of taking her clothes off bit by bit in front of the full-length mirror in her bedroom.

Her poor body is older now and her breasts are larger as they hang down on her chest, but her shapely body can still bring her much pleasure. As it will tonight.

She thinks of her late husband at this time, when he would be grabbing her from behind as she stands naked in front of the mirror. She remembers his strong hands taking pleasurable liberties with her body, and going searching between her legs.

Before he passed away—all too soon for Gertrude—Doug arranged a surprise for their 35th wedding anniversary. Gertrude remembers well the shock and confusion when she opened the foot-long box to find a very lifelike soft toy that looked exactly like her husband, dressed in his favorite casual shirt and jeans.

For a moment, she had thought that her husband had lost it. Why else would he give her a doll, and of himself no less?

When he explained to her about this special doll that he went traveled so far to have made especially for her, Gertrude was even more convinced that his mind was playing tricks on him.

Her memories of those nights are vivid. Under the light of the full moon, Doug had undressed both her and himself. Then he directed her to lie down on their bed and open her thighs.

Instead of favoring her with his attention, as Gertrude was expecting and hoping he would, Doug produced the little doll replica of himself from behind his back, and walked it up the avenue between her legs.

The curtains had been opened to let in the peaceful pearly light of the full moon. One patch of it now lit the walking soft toy.

It was as if the little man had his batteries switched on or Doug had wound him up. The little robot was walking—of its own free will—away from his husband's hands and straight towards her open vagina.

Its little pinhead of a prick was growing larger as Gertrude watched; she even saw a smile light up little Doug's face as the figure reached her cunt, which had been cleanly shaven as a surprise for her husband on their wedding anniversary.

Gertrude jumped as the little penis missed her opening and jabbed into her clitoris.

"Hell, watch it little man," she screamed.

But as soon as his little prick entered her hole, it was a signal for it to begin to grow, along with the rest of the body of the little man.

It didn't seem possible. Alarmed, Gertrude watched the little soft toy blow up like a balloon to the size of her actual husband, who was now sitting on the sofa to marvel at what was happening on the bed.

Was he being cuckolded by himself?

Although still very much doll-like, with its painted-on eyes, emotionless mouth and expressionless face, the big doll almost mechanically went about its business. Its increasingly large penis was unthinkingly screwing Gertrude, sending ripples of pleasure through her body.

The doll's dick felt very much like the real Doug's when it was at its firmest. The soft, stuffed cotton cloth had become rigid and dense, and smooth as real flesh.

Gertrude gripped the doll's body as she was reaching the edge of her mounting orgasm. Some small part of her mind noticed that its cotton covering felt like real skin. How that could be she didn't know, and at that moment she didn't really care.

Since her poor Doug had passed away six years ago, Gertrude had rarely missed an opportunity to bring out the doll. One night a month, every month, her little Doug performed his amazing mechanical fucking like a demented spirit without fail.

She also frequently arranged naughty full-moon parties with a group of local women, who otherwise met for coffee and cake one afternoon a week. Almost every month she let the little Doug loose among them to tirelessly pleasure them.

Gertrude remembered the bedlam little Doug caused the first time he trotted out in the living room, naked, his blunt sword pointing accusingly at the ladies. Their screams were worse than if a rat had dashed out and run up the skirt of one of the women.

But then the suburban ladies became used to, and even greatly anticipated, Gertrude's doll parties. Eventually, a whole host of naked dolls, male and female, would fan out from the store room, each targeting individual women.

It's often hard to believe what the sedate and dignified ladies get up to with their dolls when the parties are raging.

Back in Massachusetts, Mary can only imagine what her army of hundreds of little dolls do when they reach the homes of her Internet customers.

But the thought of her little dolls fucking, bringing pleasure and causing havoc to the lives of lonely men and women around the world makes Mary feels that her job is very worthwhile.

12 HUNTED

In her young life, Emily has always preferred to live dangerously. For her, life is far too mundane, and the days are filled only with work, shopping, and TV.

Summer is ablaze in the forests around her town of Spokane. So Emily packs her tent and other camping gear and heads off in her car to Lake Freedom, which she loves. She knows places there where she can be alone, go skinny-dipping in the lake, and stalk the bears and moose like a huntress, or really the naturalist that she is.

Emily finds her usual spot behind an old stand of pines, and pitches her small tent on the tough grass near a little coarse gravel beach at the side of the big pristine lake.

In the past she has seen big parties of hunters toting their rifles come noisily past this side of the lake, especially on weekends like this one. If they come this weekend, she might give them some sport, and herself in the process.

Emily tosses on her damp T-shirt on the roof of the tent, freeing her ample white breasts. Then she wriggles out of her tight jeans, to reveal a young and shapely body that could do with some added color from the summer sun.

As Emily dives in the lake, her full pink bottom breaks the surface with a splash that echoes in this silent wilderness. The lake water feels very cool around her thighs, and laps her dark pubic hair.

Surfacing, Emily hears men's voices, speaking loudly from the opposite forest.

Shit, hunters, thinks Emily, as she swims quietly to hide behind some large rocks.

The burly hunters, six of them, come through the trees out into the clearing where her tent is.

"Hey, this must be that spunky girl camper that we see here some times," says one of the men. "She is quite a dish and I wouldn't mind tumbling into her sleeping bag tonight." The men laugh.

"Looky here!, her clothes are on the tent!"

"She's probably skinny-dipping," says an older man. "Let her be."

"Wouldn't mind having a closer look at her, though," says the first hunter. "What's that?"

He hunter catches a glimpse of Emily's brilliant white bum skipping into the shady forest.

"Hey guys, this naked girl is running about in the forest of the other side of the lake," he yells to his mates. "Let's go and catch us a girl for supper!"

"Yeah!" say the others, as the hunters tramp her way.

Emily's bare feet are hurting as she runs swiftly through the pines. She hides behind one trunk, looks to see where her hunters are, and then dashes on to the next cover.

One member of the group looks though his binoculars and signals the others who have fanned out now and are marching in her direction.

Emily probably knows her way around this forest better than the men who have assembled from elsewhere than this district. She can easily backtrack around them and escape.

Instead she crawls under a low bush that deliciously scratches her bare skin and waits. This young hind wants to be caught.

The hunters try to move quietly, as if they are stalking a flighty deer. But any deer with any sense would have sprung well away now, from the noises of the men's movements through the shrubs.

As naked Emily couches like a frightened animal, the big rough men with their big guns were all around her, still searching.

Then the young one behind her sees her bare bottom through the leaves and sneaks up to grab her between her legs.

The men stand around her hapless position and laugh. A couple of silly ones even point their rifles at her as if ready to shoot her if she makes a dash for freedom.

"Looky here. Now that's a sight for sore

eyes," says a big man with a beard. "Stand up, girlie! Let's have a look at you."

Emily stands up tall now and looks back at the ogling men, who mostly look rather dumb to her. A couple of leering men approach and feel her breasts, the other grab at her cunt and her bottom.

Emily stands her ground and stares back.

The young man roughly ties her hands behind her back with his dirty handkerchief. Then he fondles her bottom, then her tits again. The sensation is pleasant for Emily but she doesn't make that too obvious to the guy.

The young woman hasn't said a word, but meekly follows her captors back to her tent. There the older hunter, called Peter, puts her socks and walking boots on for her while she stands. His eyes are fixed on the fuzz of her full bulging cunt directly in front of him, as a bonus.

The men take her to a disused cabin in the woods that she had previously looked inside. There they sit her on a bed in one corner of the cabin on a dirty, dank mattress. Her heart is throbbing.

The men make themselves at home, stand their rifles and bring out warm cans of beer from their backpacks to hand around.

Kindly Peter takes a can to Emily and unties her hands. Emily drinks the beer thirstily in a gulp.

The hunters now discuss who is going be first.

Peter brought out handfuls of condom packets, ordering the men to wear them. He seems to wield some authority over the guys.

Someone brings out a pack of cards, and the six men, Peter included, anxiously select a card each. The young man, Jason, who fondled Emily previously, yelps as he draws the highest card.

As the men sit drinking on chairs and some smoke, Jason takes pleasure in standing over Emily and slowly unbuckles himself, pulling out a cock as hard as a barrel of a large pistol.

He pushes Emily roughly back down on the bed and pushes her thighs open wide. As Peter watches, Jason quickly slips on his condom, and falls on top of his hapless prey.

Emily feels the full strength of his hard penis, entering deep into her. The young man is actually quite spunky, and she is enjoying his mechanical gallop.

She looks at the other men, who are absorbed in what is going on this side of the room, their eyes wide, their mouths open above their beer cans.

"Oh, fuck, fuck, fuck!" yells the young hunter as he strains to shoot off.

While Jason was still heavy on top of her, the second hunter is already in a queue behind him, impatient for Jason to get off. He ends up pulling Jason off physically.

Emily is actually wanting for the second man to start as her own concealed excitement reaches its own peak. This Number 2, with a much bigger and longer rifle of a dick, has now forced himself in so tight and hard that Emily has to scream.

That seemed to add to this brute's

enjoyment as he pushes in and out with absolute gusto. Emily in response can't hold on any longer and closes her eyes firmly and jerks as her internal atom bomb explodes to obliterate her inside.

Only Peter seems to have noticed Emily's deep orgasm, happening even before the brute's own noisy finish.

But there is no rest for poor Emily as Number 3 is already standing over them with his dick hanging out, already sheathed in rubber.

Again, he has to pull the brute Number 2 off by his shirt.

This man roughly pulls Emily and turns her over so that she kneels by the side of the bed with her delicious bottom facing the men.

She can hear them gasp in appreciation at the gash open invitation.

Number 3 is not aiming for her vagina but places his rocket directly on her anus. Emily instinctively resists by tightening her muscle, but the force being opposed is much stronger and the brutish shaft gets through and pushes right in.

"Ah, God!" screams Emily loudly. The pleasure and pain, coming soon after her previous explosion, are almost too much.

While Number 3 is pounding her relentlessly, Number 4 has also come to kneel beside her and fondles her breasts. He is no doubt mesmerized by the piston moving in her anus, which actually feels as if it is on fire. She watches Number 4 stroke his erect penis slowly, clearly enjoying the sight of her agony.

Number 3 is shouting now something unintelligible, as his rod is pushed even deeper inside Emily than she thought possible and ejaculates warm and pleasant inside her.

As the big dick is pulled out of her, Emily feels relief and longs for a longer respite. But no, the strong Number 4 has lifted her up completely off the floor so that, like some kind of inflatable sex doll, Emily's tired thighs are lifted by his arms and are being pulled open further.

She sees now that Number 5 is ready with his trousers already around his ankles. There is no escaping for Emily as Number 4 is pushing her wide-open vulva directly at the point of Number 5's thick penis.

She is now sandwiched in the middle of the cabin with the other hunters cheering them all on.

Somehow Number 4 has succeeded in inserting his smaller penis into her bottom as well and is now shoving it right in while standing up. The men work in perfect harmony to fill her holes and increase her pleasure.

Emily feels well and truly penetrated just now by two men at the same time, both struggling to get to their orgasmic blasts. If Emily wasn't so tired she would be also actively trying to get her rocks off in this unique way. The men finish and leave throw her on the bed like a used towel.

She is exhausted, but then Peter has yet to have his turn. Peter walks to Emily with his naked rod bouncing. Peter caresses her body and peppers her abdomen with soft kisses. He gently pushes her legs apart and eases his erect penis into her throbbing cunt. He eases in and out while Emily softly moans and sighs.

He comes now, as gentle as her own dad. He cradles her now protectively as she rests.

13 PHUKET'S RED LIGHTS

Chuck feels like a naughty boy as he enters the travel agent in Intercourse, PA, from the snowy street the next town from his own town of Lancaster. Not so many people know him here in this Amish town.

He had just driven his dear wife Stella to the airport to visit her sick and elderly mum in Seattle. She is to be away for three weeks.

When he sees a brochure about a very affordable week-long package tour with Thai Airways International airline to a resort island in Phuket (which he finds damned hard to pronounce, by the way), Chuck is convinced. The pamphlet is full of unbelievably beautiful girls and transvestites who are just waiting for his arrival, it seems.

The dowdy travel agent girl sneaks suspicious looks at him as she prepares his ticket, but by now he doesn't care. Hasn't the girl seen an aging, God-fearing sex tourist before? But then not all that many Amish men are your eager sex tourists, jetting off to Thailand, he doesn't expect.

Chuck can't believe his eyes when he steps on the big THAI jumbo at LA airport. If the Phuket (sounds like Fuckit, doesn't it?) bar girls are half as pretty as these hostesses, then he will be a busy and happy man.

As he sits drinking a Thai Chang beer (which is pretty good beer really), Chuck reaches into his trouser pocket and feels his stirring cock, as one of the stunning ladies walks past and smiles at him.

You lucky son of a gun, he thinks. "Let's fuck one Thai girl every day while we are in Thailand," he tells his horny companion.

From America that is crisply under snow, Chuck walks into a tropical oven, as he leaves the small airport building. One attractive girl, actually a tranny, carries a big card with his name written on it.

The tourist van drives fast and crazily on the long and hilly road to Patong, a too-popular destination holiday town by the sea. From his beach-side hotel room, Chuck sees a crowded beach and a long esplanade packed with cars, little taxis, and a million shoppers.

As soon as he drops his bags in the hotel room, the sex tourist is off to Bangla Road in the middle of Patong.

He decides immediately that the road's name should be Hell Street, as it consists of just one red-light bar after another, overflowing with bevies of bar girls and transvestites in the skimpiest of skirts and hot pants and tight tops, as he has seen in the brochure.

Many of these sex workers were dancing on top of bars and other high perches, pushing their pelvis more than suggestively around poles as they dance around them, accompanied by loud music.

"Ping-Pong, sir?" asks one tout after another of both sexes. "Ping-Pong show, very good!" they promise, sticking their thumbs up.

Who's he to argue? Chuck is led into an air-conditioned backroom of a bar that was crowded with Western men and their Thai girls. There is an empty couch in the middle of the room as the gyrating music starts.

Two stunning lithe girls, wearing their pink and white bikini tops and G-strings, dance slowly to the couch, deliciously stripping the few clothes that they have along the way and flicking them into the applauding audience.

Chuck has only seen bodies like these on Net porn sites, so now he is just drinking it all in. The girls with their long straight black hair now drape themselves at either end of the couch, opening their marvelous legs, facing each other, to show their cunts that have been shaven smooth.

To Chuck's utter surprise, one tight vagina on the left shoots out a pink Ping-Pong ball which bounces on the floor and rolls out into the audience. The vagina on the right also answers with its own concealed white ball which pops out and also bounces into the audience, to claps and laughter.

Oye, the name of the prettier Ping-Pong player, means sugarcane in Thai. And Chuck tastes that sweetness in both her kisses and her demeanor.

Just a whispered word from Chuck to the tout and the price is agreed at the usual 2,000 baht (US $60) for the night, and the young bar girl comes to him after the show.

The two treated themselves to supper ordered to their luxurious room while they wait, gazing out to the night sea that reflects moonlight. When food is delivered, he locks the door.

Then, without too many words exchanged, as Oye speaks very broken English, she lets Chuck slip off the few items of clothing she has from her nubile body.

For Chuck, it's like opening a Christmas present, the first of seven that he plans to give himself. Her firm small breasts with their erect jet-black nipples nestle well in his big palms and feel glorious.

The slope of her full stomach curves down to a cute small mound of sex, dramatically exposing her clean-shaven area for her Ping-Pong matches.

She rather expertly undresses her American customer too—as no doubt she has many others before him of all nationalities—so that his pink-white portly body, big penis, and scrotum sac hang down in the tropical night.

They eat hungrily as it has been a long day for both. Oye's large black eyes are always on Chuck, happy and enquiring. Her lusty full lips smile often.

Oye drains the last of her chilled Chardonnay and is ready for work. She moves from her side of the table to mount Chuck as he sits on his chair, her wonderful round legs astride his big thighs.

She holds his penis that is rising fast to greet her cunt and actually rub the brown crack in her vulva with it. "Me say welcome to Phuket, Mr. Chuck," she says with a sweet sugary smile.

Poor Mr. Chuck is bursting from the days of anticipation and can't wait. He grabs the cheeks of her firm small bottoms, lifting her to the end of the big soft bed and laying her down on her back, her thighs spread apart.

Then he falls on her, half expecting that his big American dong will not fit into the tiny Thai hole in front of him.

But it's a delectable tight fit which grabs his dick much more firmly than he has ever felt before with any other women.

As he plows her quicker now, he is surprised by Oye's response. Not only is her vagina regularly squeezing his long dick in time to his movement, heightening his pleasure immensely, but also she herself seems to be transported by their fucking.

As Chuck releases his pent-up energy in a wild throbbing burst, so does Oye reach her peak, making a strange long high-pitched trailing sound and shuddering all over her body.

The hard-working girl rests for a while after that, her body entwined around his big limbs. As jet-lagged Chuck dozes, he is woken two or three more times in the night by Oye sucking on his prick to wake it up or by her small hand caressing and squeezing his genitals.

When he wakes the next morning, more than well sated from the previous night pleasure, Oye is gone, no doubt to rest and get ready for her next Ping-Pong tournament.

Oye was amused by Chuck's fucking quest when he told her. But as she didn't seem to think that it was anything unusual, Chuck's horny project may not be that original after all in this place.

For Chuck's next lay, Oye suggests her good friend Maeow, who can be found at night in Mick's Aussie Bar.

There she is alright, dancing listlessly around a shiny pole on a bar in a dim red-lit corner, again on Hell Street, while the Aussie blokes, mostly beer-bellied and white-haired, talk loudly among themselves and pay her little heed.

Of the same height and build as Oye, Maeow has more flesh with bigger breasts and bum, with tummy bulging invitingly above her tiny glittering bikini.

She smiles at Chuck straightaway, probably expecting him. Chuck enjoys his luxury of leaning back on his soft seat in a dark corner, listening to the driving music and appreciating her smooth suggestive gyration, now performed directly for him.

The bulge of her pubic mound under the G-string, pushing out in his direction, has him mesmerized. Hers is bigger than Oye's. Will it be bare and free of concealing hair as well? Chuck can hardly stand the suspense.

He thinks briefly of Stella. If only she can see him now. He'll make it up to her using the different fucking tricks that he is learning from the Thai pros. There will be some nice homing welcomes for her.

The hotel female receptionists are looking at them now as Chuck and his number 2 walk past, trying to be nonchalant.

Knowing more English than Oye, Maeow, meaning cat in Thai, chats away easily, seeming happy to have a client she can relate to.

After her shower, which she didn't want to share with her man, Chuck finds her waiting for him, curled up in a crouched position like a cat on top of the big bed, her round delectable bottom pointing invitingly in his direction.

Like a big tomcat, Chuck mounts her straightaway, his penis sheathed in protective rubber and searching for its tight-fitting home.

"Not there, Mister," meows the Cat, "Here!"

She deftly inserts with her hand the bulging tip of Chuck's penis into her anus. "Go, man, go in."

Chuck by this time is beside himself. No woman has ever let him do this before, let alone inviting him in her through her tight back passage. What his penis is feeling is truly overwhelming.

The sex tourist can see his hard shaft slowly sliding in through the dark puckered opening. Watching all the while with his hands grabbing either side of her firm round bottom, Chuck is halfway to the heaven that his church pastor talks of at home.

He is able to repeat his rear attack twice more this night when Maeow is almost asleep by turning her over gently, climbing over to position, and pushing his big oiled tool into her bottom.

Last time, he also filled in her cunt crack in the front while gently breaching her anus leisurely, and for a long time, Chuck is proud to be able to bring the sleepy Cat to a mounting, meowing orgasm at the same time as his own ecstatic and draining one, the combined noises of which are probably enough to wake people up in the next room.

Before slipping out of the hotel room in the morning, Maeow also recommended a friend in another bar.

Meanwhile, Chuck spends the morning in bed, looking out to the sea where fishing boats are returning from the night's fishing.

In another life, he can very well live here in the same carefree and economical way that many of the American, English, and Russian expatriates that he has met are doing. They hold Thai retirement visas that are easy to get, and many are living well on their savings and pensions from back home.

Can he simply stay on here and forget about returning? Poor Stella.

He notices Jai as soon as he enters the crowded bar. She is sitting among the spare girls who are not with customers at the moment, her unique beauty shining forth across the room.

The two sneak away quickly from the noisy place, walking down little smelly alleys and on paths through dark rubber trees in a plantation, to Jai's small wooden house.

Jai, meaning heart in Thai, introduces him to her two young children from her previous marriage to a Thai man, who are being looked after by her mother.

After a good meal with the family and after the children have gone to bed in grandma's room upstairs, the couple retire to Jai's bedroom at the back of the house.

Under the cover of the darkness of the rubber trees, the two undress each other and step outside to bathe from a big earthenware urn, splashing over each other with cool water from little plastic hand scoops.

Under the dim starlight, Chuck' s large white hands were soaping the shapely body of Jai, which, for Chuck, comes close to the perfection of female beauty as he has ever seen.

Jai has not tampered with her lovely body at all: there is hair in her arm pits and a full soft black bush between her full thighs.

Seeing Chuck' dick sticking up in the direction of the top of the rubber trees, Jai smiles and leans back on the wet urn, opens her wonderful thighs, and lowers the big American space-shuttle rocket to her opening.

For Chuck, his entry into her feels like returning home, like the home that the more spacious vagina of Stella also provides. He feels that he can stay in there forever or return to this home again and again anytime.

Jai is holding her soft body to him as if he were some kind of savior. For a good change, she actually reaches her orgasm well before his. She muffles her cries but is unable to control the wild undulation of her body and her head that knocks repeatedly into Chuck's chest.

Chuck feels good to be able to do that with his sturdy rod before it decides to shoot off its own load.

Under the mosquito net on Jai's soft double bed, Chuck is mostly content to finish more gently once again between Jai's homely legs and to rest there on top of the poor woman, his dick in a pool of sperm discharged into her vagina.

He helps her wipe up later, then remembers that at her age, Jai may still need protection against unwanted pregnancy that he didn't provide.

As he cradles her, listening to the rustling of rubber leaves and the distant early crowing of a rooster, Chuck feels strangely at home.

As he absentmindedly caresses against Jai's soft breasts, belly, and the moist jungle between her legs, Jai wakes up. She turns to him to curl back to sleep, murmuring, "Stay with me, Chuck. Stay here with us."

For Chuck just now, visions of the mundane street and snow-covered wheat fields of Lancaster and Intercourse are far away. So is the familiar shop front of his locksmith business—and the notice on its door that he is taking a week off.

He sees his blond and chubby Stella, his dull but loving companion for decades, waving to him soon as she walks through the airport arrival gate.

As the sky pales with the first rays of Phuket's sun, Chuck again climbs on top and between the legs of Jai, who is still fast asleep. He needs to feel again what his new home is like: it's soft, warm, welcoming, and waiting for him.

"Hey, Chuck, you are horny. Can never get enough?" mumbles Jai, whose sleepy eyes are still not open. "But that's good. There is plenty for you here at this place," Jai says while trying to fall back to sleep again.

Chuck fucks away, gently, almost like caressing her inside, as Jai dozes on.

He is a sex tourist after all.

14 BONDI GIRL

Footloose and fancy free, American Felicity finds herself at Bondi beach in Sydney at the start of her two-year working holiday in Australia. The girl finds freedom that she has never experienced before, spending long halcyon days in the sunny suburb and at the famous beach. The hot Australian summer nights are filled with fucking partners, male and female, a fun way for Felicity to get to know a new country.

This Australian beach bum has got stamina. There he is again on top of her and really going hammers and tongs between Felicity's legs, this early in the morning, after such a hectic night.

Felicity doesn't know how her cunt will be after such an onslaught. Admittedly, this handsome find of hers knows how to fuck a girl, and Felicity had her fill of satisfying thrashing about last night. And here he is again, working away above her, going for it, just as another summer sky is lightening outside.

Felicity knows only that this tanned muscular hunk man, with his cool mop of bleached blond hair, is called Geoff, and he came from the bush to surf at Bondi for a while.

In her couple of months or so at this fantastic iconic place, Felicity has met and fucked a few men who have come to this famous beach "to surf for a while" and obviously to fuck a few women on the loose like her, also "for a while".

The girl is too sleepy to let herself go to another orgasm, so she enjoys seeing her blond lover have his, as he soon crashes on top of her afterwards.

She strokes his back that is packed with muscles, feels his hard bum, and thanks her lucky stars for bringing her to this freedom beach where there is unending summer.

As Felicity walks around the little streets leading to the roaring beach in the early morning or late afternoon, she soaks the sun-filled, carefree life that is to be had everywhere. As always, the sky high and blue and the pale yellow wattles are ablaze against it.

The money she earns from working as a

waitress in a cool bar for three days at the weekend is enough to pay rent for her neat little bed-sit flat on the second floor with a glimpse of the distant blue sea.

Much of the time then is free, a liberty that Felicity has rarely felt, if ever, even back home, in that land of the free.

Under the beach umbrella that she can hire, the American lass can take off her bikini top and shift to sit in the sun for a while to get an overall tan. Many gorgeous women go topless on this beach, their bulbous breasts swinging sweaty and often alarmingly overcooked by the sun.

And the women may as well go bottomless, for the amount that their G-string bikini bottoms cover. Felicity loves to admire their large "arses," as Australians say, flopping and wobbling everywhere, or simply being proudly shapely.

Felicity notices her lesbian lover immediately from far. The word butch described this girl very well, in a nice way. She is rather plumb with small pert tits that she has bared to join others on the blazing sand, against the background of the roaring big surf.

This butch girl walks in a very manly and commanding way. Her round face is pretty. She also connects with Felicity from far away on the big crowded beach and marches straight up the beach to the American girl.

"Hi! I'm Jan. Are you lesbian?" she asks, nothing if not direct.

"No, but please sit down, if you are," says Felicity with her best smile.

Jan lays down next to Felicity in the shade of the umbrella so that the nipples of her small breasts touch Felicity's arm. Then the lesbian's finger begins to slowly trace the contour of Felicity's body, starting from her navel.

The traveling finger follows the top of the full round hill and slope of the tummy down to the tight white bikini bottom. There it traces the contour of the top of the small mound of Venus and follows the dip of the valley in the middle, to pass the time.

Later in Jan's ram-shackled apartment, the same butch fingers again explore Felicity's tanned body that is now fully naked. This time, they spend a lot of time in the moist Venus valley, as if to gently draw the outline of Felicity's clitoris, the sink hole of her vagina and her tight anus.

Apart from playful petting with her sisters and female friends, Felicity has never really made love to another woman. But with Jan, all is very sensual and natural.

At one stage in the night though, Jan's full and fragrant, not to say pungent, hairy pussy is squashing squarely on Felicity's mouth as Jan gets worked up from Felicity's sucking and licking her clitoris.

Felicity finds later that when Jan is after her orgasm, she goes for it with all guns blazing. So now, she is rubbing and grinding her wet open vulva on Felicity's mouth and nose, with increasing ferocity and urgency, as Jan straddles and pins her poor partner on the bed.

As Jan's strong big thighs are squeezing her face, Felicity does all she can to keep breathing, while enjoying both the sight and sound of this rampant lesbian in full gallop.

Jan, on the other hand, doesn't forget her partner in return and has turned around a little later to straddle the other way and buried her face into Felicity's open cunt.

Jan's practiced licking and sucking very soon sends Felicity off, her lower-half pushing up and her torso struggling, to the sight of Jan's big active bum straddling in front of her.

Felicity doesn't know what mood has got hold of her tonight. Stopping late at her usual kebab store on the beach road for the favorite supper of lamb kebab on her way back to her apartment from work, she is enjoying the cooler night air under the stars.

The walkway to the beach at this point tunnels under the road that is usually busy, but is deserted now. As Felicity walks towards it, alarm bells ring in her mind. She knows that the broad beach is on the other side where the tunnel becomes some nice bold mural art.

But it's after midnight, and the way is as

dark as can be. Is she soft in the head? Dare she? It could be suicidal with all the riff-raffs and drug addicts who live on Sydney streets.

She does dare.

At the mouth of the dark tunnel, Felicity takes off all her work clothes and stuffs them all in her carry bag, leaving only her sneakers to walk on. She ambles briskly, totally naked, into the darkness.

There are now only sounds of her footsteps and the surf from the other side of the tunnel. Freedom. But surely, this is going too far and too risky. But Felicity feels good with her heart throbbing and adrenalin flowing.

With luck, it would be too late in the night for anybody to be in her way.

But Felicity now hears men talking in the darkness. Too late, she just has to walk on. Two burly stocky beach men, dressed only in swim briefs, are chatting at the end of the tunnel.

Felicity quickens her steps and heads for the narrow space between them.

The expressions on the face of the foreign men when they see her are comical, if the situation was less threatening.

"Allah protects us," one Middle Eastern man says. "Hey, slow down, nude sheila. Pretty dangerous to be walking around like that at this time of night."

"Would you believe this?" the second man says to his companion. "We better give her some protection."

They stand together to block Felicity's way.

"I still can't believe this, can you, mate?" he says to his companion.

"Naw," says the other. "New one on me, mate. What will we do with her?"

The men have sandwiched Felicity between them, thick hairy arms linking to stop her.

"Please let me through," says Felicity, more alarmed.

One man's rough hand is already grabbing the cheeks of her bum. Another hand is grabbing her breast.

"Wow, feel this, mate. This here is something. Let's take this exhibitionist to that grassy patch there and see what she is made of?"

Each grabbing her by one arm, they push Felicity onto her back on the cool grass. They both stand over each of her legs, ready to stop her escaping.

They slip down their brief swimmers to reveal large penises hanging down from black hairy growths.

"Hold on, boys. You'll get into real trouble with the police this way," says Felicity hastily. "How about escorting me home, and I'll make you supper, we drink some wine together, and fuck, even together, if you like."

The men look at each other and pull up their swimmers again, smiling broadly.

"You're on, girlie," one says.

The men actually help Felicity put her clothes back on. As the three walk to Felicity's place, one of the men casually draping an arm around her shoulder and

Felicity thinks that this is one hell of a novel way to pick up men.

The apartment's little bathroom is filled with steam and two hunky men who are at Felicity's disposal. Sensuously quashed between their thickset bodies with the men big palms soaping literally every nook and cranny of her body, Felicity is enjoying herself immensely.

She lets a waterfall of gushing warm rain wash away the suds that the men have spent long delicious moments making with cakes of soap in all parts of her body.

All the while, the hairy men's thick penises seem to grow even larger, both inviting Felicity to feel their hard shafts with both hands.

"Wow, wow," is all that she is able to say, as she handles one and then the other, marveling at these sturdy baby and orgasm making instruments.

There is a big cock pointing up and pressing hard on her tummy. So it's relatively easy for Felicity to stretch herself up, open her legs, and ease the soapy upright minaret into her.

"God is great," murmurs Affendi, as his rod tightly squeezes in. Felicity too agrees that his God is great as she has actually never felt such a male muscle so tightly inside her before.

Then comes also hard probing from behind from Abdullah's equally gorged penis. It's pushing in between the cheeks of her bottom.

"Whoah, man. Hold on!" cries the poor girl. "...I don't think that's a good idea."

"Relax girl," comes a firm voice from behind, as the head of the big bludgeon finds the tight opening of her anus and is pushing relentlessly in.

"Yikes! God Almighty," says Felicity as she is lifted by two penises pushing up into her two openings. "Easy, boys, yikes!"

It now seems an eternity in that steam cloud, with Felicity very much the meat in the middle of a struggling sandwich before firstly Affendi then very soon afterwards Abdullah reach their mighty climaxes, both growling and groaning loudly like wild animals.

Felicity herself may have reached hers along the way but is mostly too busy trying to keep from being torn asunder.

Tired from her shower for three, Felicity is resting in her bed for three. She is in a warm nest with the men collapsing on either side of her.

"You know we're gay?" says Affendi casually to her before they fall asleep as three innocent children sharing the same bed.

Later in the night, Felicity awakes to the sight of her two lovers making love between them. She learns how gentle it can be for two big men to kiss and cuddle each other in this most natural way.

It also feels unusual that a woman is for a change not the focus of attention of these men who actually seem to have no need for women at all.

Felicity's favorite time is to go to Aaron who teaches her violin twice a week.

Many Jewish immigrants from Russia for some reason prefer to live in Bondi, and Aaron lives in a picturesque ancient apartment with a balcony that catches the sun and the constant salty breeze from the sea.

When he plays pieces from Bach or Beethoven, in the big carpeted living room, Felicity just sinks away in a big armchair, lost to the music.

The lonely old man has lived by himself for some years after his wife passed away. He has become like a grandpa to her, but one who always has room in his bed for her.

Felicity remembers well the first time the handsome and aristocratic man first touched her. It was like in a movie or a book. As she was playing her violin, Aaron was walking around adjusting the best posture for her arms and back.

The student then felt the teacher gently grabbing her waist and then from behind fondling her breasts with both sensitive hands of a musician. Then the firm hands felt further down her stomach and fondled her cunt, effectively halting her scale practice.

Aaron profusely apologized, saying that it must have been the music that got to him.

In reply, Felicity actually reached to kiss his forehead, feeling pity and fondness for the old guy.

Aaron cooked good kosher food for supper, changed into striped pajamas, and waited in his big bed.

The young student in the meantime took off all her clothes, danced the ballet steps that took her back to childhood lessons, and then neatly slipped into bed with her teacher.

There, the student was also a teacher in some ways, said Aaron. That night, and many times since then, Felicity rode on the ageing penis that still had enough strength left in it. She enjoyed seeing Aaron studying her wide open thighs and neat young cunt that is riding away with determination on his cock in front of him.

Since those earlier times, not that long ago actually, Felicity has become very fond of the old maestro. She always looks forward to her lessons that actually give her the chance to spend nights at the old apartment with its distant sounds of the beloved beach.

Aaron's place has become a harbor to return to from all her wild suburban wanderings at the pounding beach.

Lately, to please the maestro a little more, this student takes off all her clothes and plays all her homework pieces back to him in the nude.

Aaron has the pleasure to sit and enjoy both the sight and sound of his student playing au natural in the middle of his large living room.

And he has a surprise for her tonight.

Felicity finds a big bunch of red roses on their supper table along with the usual glasses of red wine. The old man is all dressed up as he serves her more delicious food, lovingly cooked.

What's up?

"Dear Felicity, my good student and bed partner, would you like to do me the honor of marrying me and living with me here?" asks Aaron formally, his voice is quiet and his eyes are kind.

"Yes, Aaron, I would," Felicity replies, also formally and without hesitation, knowing for some time that something like this was in the offering.

Naked in bed with a man twice her age that night, Felicity found him even more tender and exciting. She wraps her arms and legs around his sleeping body even more tightly.

Out in the Bondi summer night, and no doubt busy in their life's searching, are Geoff, Jan, Affendi, and Abdullah.

Her own search has also been long and adventurous, since she left her home in San Francisco. With the help of dear Aaron and Bondi beach, Felicity has found a new home by another sea.

15 STREETWALKER

Stunning blond Ukranian woman Anushka has left her drunken good-for-nothing husband back home. She didn't expect to receive a visa to travel to the US by herself. But once she has entered the land of hope and opportunity, she tears up her return plane ticket. But to try to live in this new country, she has to walk the street of New York as a beautiful prostitute, who comes to meet a dream customer.

Anushka stands at her favorite corner of Central Park, where there is a little pull-in for cruising cars to stop. It is bitterly cold, and it looks like more snow will fall tonight to top up what is already on the ground and on the dark park trees.

Snuggled up well in her good coat and a thick Russian mink fur hat, Anushka could be back home on the frozen wasteland streets of St. Petersburg, or in her small home village in the Ukraine.

She has a very short woolen skirt on underneath her coat with plenty of room to show the customers her long legs and thighs from underneath.

But home is far away, and she is very glad of that. Her good-for-nothing, violent, and drunken Boris is also far away, and good riddance to bad rubbish.

A long and expensive-looking black car approaches and slows down for a long inspection. Anushka makes sure that her beautiful face, framed by long golden hair, can be seen in the street light. A bare pale leg is also casually showing from under the coat.

The car cruises by, its windows too dark to see inside. Some moments later, it comes back in the floating snow to park next to her.

The chauffeur opens his window and signals to her to open the back door and get in. The car cruises off straightaway.

"Can you just ride with me in this lonely city for a while," says the older man with an accent, who surprisingly looks like Anushka's favorite actor of old, Omar Sharif.

In fact, she is not at all sure now that it's not the actor, who she has read is living in a hotel in Paris. This man is slightly older with a grey beard but has the same good looks.

"Yes, of course. But put your hand here please, and I can put my hand here, to keep them warm," says the streetwalker, her English still thick with Russian pronunciation.

Anushka puts the man's hand on her big thigh then moves it under her ultra-short skirt to the warmth of her crotch. She pulls down her brief panties and places his hand on the bulge of her cleanly shaven Ukranian vulva.

"How is that?" she asks.

"Oh, so wonderful," says the man quietly. If he is not the actor, maybe he is an Egyptian diplomat, perhaps posted to the UN.

"If you keep your hand there, mine will go here, and we can ride to wherever," says Anushka, expertly unzipping his fly and snaking her hand into hold the man's limp but growing penis.

Then she places her head on his shoulder and closes her eyes, feeling the warm cock in her hand hardening.

The man's fingers are gently probing and rubbing at the top of her thighs.

In that winter urban wilderness, the car cruises on. Her customer has not asked her to do it, but Anushka's head is now in his lap. Her mouth is around the round top of his penis, and she begins to suck it.

Somehow, this is different from the nocturnal routine service for her many customers. She wants to do it for this man whether he pays her for it or not, as they have not discussed money.

The man's right hand is now combing and lovingly handling her fine long blond hair. It grabs a handful of hair now hard as the man strains to ejaculate warm semen into her mouth.

"Allah al Akbar," the man whispers. God is great. Anushka sees the chauffeur averting his eyes from the rear-view mirror; he had probably been watching.

"Thank you. If you normally stand where you were tonight, may I come by again?" he asks, gazing with his gentle eyes.

"Yes, of course, that's my place of work." Anushka smiles back, sneaking a kiss on his cheek, as the man slips a roll of money in her coat pocket.

The limousine stops at the same corner of the park where she was picked up, and this time, the chauffeur, in his neat uniform, steps out to open the door for her. The car glides away again into the snowy night.

As gentle snowflakes float down in the street light, the streetwalker counts her money. There is more than enough there for her night's work budget, so she can walk back home out of the cold for an early night.

Anushka remembers her first days in this new country.

The kindly Immigration Officer at the airport gave her a long look, and it seemed an eternity before he stamped her passport.

The fact that she could get a visa to come was in itself God's gift.

Walking in Central Park in the sun among the beds of brilliant spring flowers, Anushka easily decided that this free and wonderful country was going to be her new home, regardless of the one-month tourist visa stamped in her passport.

The previous night, she had written her farewell to her drunken husband. May God keep the poor sod.

From those first heady days, Anushka decided that the only way for her to stay, without a visa and work permit, was to make full use of her good looks and make them pay their way.

Walking out from her small dingy basement apartment, dressed either in tight pants or short skirts and tight T-shirts, showing long perfect legs, the Russian blond enjoyed the visible ripples that she created as she strolled down the street.

Her black neighbor Joe was the first to propose to pay her for sex. He would knock on the door, showing whatever few dollars that he had and wanted to grab and fuck Anushka straightaway. So she let him.

In his rush, it was not often that they made it to her creaking single bed. Sometimes, it was in the dark passageway behind her door when his monster of a black cock forced its way pass her underwear deep inside her while Anushka was pinned against the wall.

Or, while starting to prepare her dinner, Anushka had to bend over the kitchen sink for the hulking black man to fuck her hard from behind, in the basement of her kitchen that can be seen from the pavement above.

Then word quickly got around that the sexy Ukranian in her basement flat is on the job. There were gentle knocks on her door day and night at odd times, and Anushka always opened up to let the lonely guys in.

It was also good way to practice English and get to know Americans who are really not all that different from anyone at home.

For a breath of fresh air, more than anything, Anushka walked the streets in the evening, going down different smaller ones, heading for the park. Cars stop and drivers ask her price, so she just names it, according to how she likes the look of a particular customer.

With others, warning bells sound and the streetwalker just walks on, ignoring them.

And what varied customers she has satisfied: Blacks, Jews, Muslims, diplomats, lawyers and even a judge, she thinks, and also lesbian women.

Even Paddy the policeman managed to get in on the act. Walking his beat one hot summer night, he chatted to Anushka as usual, but this once also made an offer that she could not refuse.

He wanted to pay for her service on the lawn behind some bush in Central Park. So then there was the streetwalker on the ground with her lovely thighs open to the policeman standing over her between her legs.

He removed his belt with its long lethal

truncheon, big revolver, and handcuffs, and stashed them with his hat safely nearby. Paddy took his time fucking her, no doubt enjoying himself in this break from the routine night watch.

As the law enforcer struggled to cum, Anushka heard voices and saw a couple of black lovers looking in with startled white eyes, and then scurrying away.

For all of her customers, the prostitute gave her best, using all the tricks and tools of her new trade, and she was happy when customers returned for second and third helpings from the honey pot.

Anushka is overjoyed when mysterious Omar Sharif comes back. Again, the limousine just appears out of the night, quite late.

This night, she is invited to the man's plush apartment where a fine supper and champagne are waiting on a dining table. The apartment looks out to snow-covered Central Park down below.

"Will you stay with me here and be my mistress?" says her man eventually. His name, he says, is actually Omar.

"I have prepared a nice part of the apartment for you, that I'll show you later."

"Yes, Omar, of course," says Anushka. She is surprised at her own quick agreement.

"May I ask a few things of you, though? Are you always naked within your apartment, which is well-heated, and preferably out here too? I entertain business associates from time to time, and it would be nice if you help me to entertain them too, still always showing your gorgeous body undressed. I will pay you well, of course, for that extra service."

Omar continued, "Also there is an Egyptian belly-dancer coming in to teach you how to belly-dance. If you can learn it well, you can dance for me and also my guests. My wife and the children will sometime visit me here from Cairo. Maybe, only then should you put some clothes on! How does that sound?" Omar asks.

"Good! Maybe except for the belly-dancing!" says Anushka, in her thick accent and laughing. "A Ukranian peasant girl belly-dancing? Are you sure about that?"

"We'll see. Anything is possible in my place," says Omar, smiling his charming smile and glancing around. "The driver will fetch your things and you won't need to go back to your flat."

"How can I thank you, Omar?" asks the former streetwalker and now mistress.

"Oh, I'm sure you have ways," says Omar with a smile.

The man shows her to her new spacious and stylish quarters, the likes of which she has only seen in Hollywood movies. She would not have been surprised to see a celebrity waltzing about in there.

As specified by Omar, Anushka drops her

short streetwalker dress and undresses completely at the door to her place.

Omar himself, an after-dinner whiskey in hand, sits back to admire his new acquisition as she prances around like a perfect thoroughbred Arabic mare.

He has some priceless nude drawings by Ingres in his bedroom, but he swears to himself that this Ukranian body with its perfectly shaped and substantial thighs and bottom, outshines the Spanish artist's visions.

That night, Omar is able to test ride his newly acquired mare, mounting Anushka from behind as she kneels in the middle of her big bed, showing her devastating bottom and her shaven cunt through her thighs.

Omar is a skillful and considerate lover. He is gentle and soft, yet able to stay the distance to hold on for a woman to have her fulfillment, too.

Being ridden well, Anushka has the luxury of feeling everything that is happening, and to let herself drift with the waves of sensation.

She grabs Omar's penis with her vagina, a technique that she knows from experience sends men wild. Secretly, it was also her way to make the paying encounters finish quicker.

In no time at all, Omar is thanking his God again as his grimacing face is pointing to the sky. Anushka has timed herself exquisitely well to let herself finish at the same time as her lover on top of her bottom.

Later in the night, she is riding him in

return, pushing Omar into the luxurious bed, and from above enjoying seeing her man becoming eventually overwhelmed.

Harem

Anushka reigns happily over her one-woman harem, going around from morning to night completely naked. She sits in the nude at the table on the occasional lunch and dinner with her man, while the Spanish cook serving their meals pretends not to see her nakedness.

The first entertainment night for Omar's business acquaintances comes around quickly.

A group of four Japanese businessmen arrive, complete with a lot of bowing all around. After dinner, Anushka, dressed in a stunning black low-cut dress, proves to be a very popular blond geisha who towers over her guests.

After dinner, as the men drink more sake and whiskey, a simply gorgeous young Egyptian belly dancer sways and gyrates her full belly and round bottom, in flowing veils that teasingly covers and uncovers parts of her body.

Then Anushka in her harem has to somehow top that erotic belly dance. With her door ajar and the lights dimmed, she waits naked on the bed, as she does most nights for Omar.

But tonight, invited by Omar, a stocky and drunk Japanese man comes in through the door, probably the boss who normally takes the first bite. Speaking little English, he gets straight to the point, undressing and vigorously mounting Anushka while making strange noises.

One after another, his underlings then come in, taking their turns and watching each other in action while enjoying their American—or is it Russian?—team-building effort.

Thank you, America.

The next morning, with her harem cleared of drunk and naked Japanese men, Anushka steps out naked into the bracing cold air to sit on her balcony, high above Central Park as the sun warms her.

The Russian immigrant sits back on her chair and opens her legs to her new country. Anushka wants to thank both America and her cunt for her good life now.

The old man Bill is sitting with his wife near the frozen pond in Central Park in their usual morning routine before they have breakfast. It looks like this morning they can sit longer as the welcoming warm sun is shining.

As usual, Bill has his binoculars to look at the squirrels digging in the snow for buried acorns and the birds hunting for breakfast on dark bare branches.

While focusing on one bird, Bill cannot believe what he is seeing in the background through his binoculars. High on a balcony near the top of a fancy apartment building, he sees the naked bottom of a woman pointing back down at him.

The gorgeous woman is all naked and is kneeling against a chair on the balcony with her lovely long blond hair flowing down her back and flopping on her face. Such a perfect body old Bill has rarely seen, all bright and golden in the sunlight, like a Playboy center spread that he has hidden away at home.

Believe it or not, the woman is masturbating all by herself on that balcony in this freezing weather.

"What kind of bird is it, dear?" asks his wife Janet. "Looks like a blackbird."

"Er... yes it is, dearie," he replies.

Focusing a little more, Bill can clearly see the woman's hand rubbing her cunt while her devastating bottom is pointing up and all open to the sun.

"Whoah," he can't help saying.

"What is it doing, dear?" asks Janet.

"Looking for a mate, I think, dearie," Bill stammers.

"Mating? Must mean then that spring is not too far away," says Janet.

"Nope, guess not," says Bill. Not for this spectacular woman anyway, he thinks.

Clearly, she is having a big orgasm right now with her lovely face grimacing and her body moving about.

"Well, I'll be damned," says Bill, as he puts his binoculars in its case. "Time to go, back for breakfast, honey?"

"Alright," says Janet. Bill seems a little agitated just now. Maybe they should go back to bed after breakfast and do some mating themselves, she thinks.

16 PASTOR'S FAVORITE

For Pastor Mary, the weekends are a good time. She loves her job of being a shepherdess for this small community of God-worshiping and God-fearing people in wheat-and-corn-belt country.

She has a neat little white-painted wooden church that is open all the time for the villagers to call in to pray privately to God.

Its location is picturesque. It sat near the forest with a little green cemetery in the back, sloping down from the forest to the back of the church, where generations of the town's people are buried.

But Pastor Mary has her own continuing, and losing, battle with Lucifer. Almost every night, her battle is lost again and again, despite all her prayers and mortification.

She blames it on the legacy of her wild and wayward youth, when she was the young slut of her community, fortunately in a different, smaller town from here.

To pardon the use of the word, but there wasn't a pimply young man in that town that she has not fucked, at one time or another. All the men around, young and old, knew about her, and for many, her young welcoming cunt was their first gateway to sex.

If that is what nymphomaniacs do, she definitely was one of those.

Oh yes, she was one of the Devil's best workers before she became a better worker for his opponent. But try as she might, she can't beat Lucifer and his overwhelming temptation of the flesh that he compels all earthly weaklings to follow.

Every day, without fail, Mary lets the Devil take hold of her hands and fingers and use them to explore her vulnerable body. Of course, he and she like to go straight to the point, targeting her clitoris in his caressing of the soft recesses of her cunt.

He uses her own experience of pleasing that marvelous fleshy switch of hers to instantly send her gaga. Her/his index fingers know exactly how to ring and press that button until her whole body is totally agitated.

And at those cliff-hanging moments, she always calls on God, and sometimes Jesus, but not the Devil, who is probably solely responsible for bringing her to those points.

But lately, she can also blame Samuel for doing that.

Just about the best part of her work

happens on Sunday morning when her whole congregation fills her little sunny church.

As she praises the work of God and his son Jesus in her sermon, the pastor enjoys seeing their individual faces that she knows so well, seeing the hope and faith on those faces that look back at her.

The tall, handsome, and black Samuel Johnson and his white American wife are new arrivals, moving to the rural community from Chicago. Mr. Johnson has come to be the new manager of the town's only bank.

Mary knows that it's a very perverse thing for her to do, but the gorgeous black manager has become her imaginary lover to help along with her nightly masturbation sessions before bed.

Also not in the textbook at her theological school is her nightly visit to her favorite site on the Internet. There, she can take her pick of the hundreds of men who are there to display all that they have for her to see.

Mary loves to marvel at the black men. Since she had never fucked one in her home town, where just about all the men are pale white, Mary and her girlfriends used to discuss at length the rumored size of African American penises.

Just the thought of the formidable equipment was enough to send Mary off, as it was for countless of times back in those wild and reckless days of her youth.

To add to the spice of black men is the pervasive Middle American taboo of any interracial connection. In those times, no white girls would date black boys, and they especially wouldn't let themselves be fucked by them.

Mary was sure that privately her girlfriends fantasized about all sorts of sex with black men, as she herself does now. But what she sees on the Internet is a real eye-opener.

Mary remembers her excitement she had a while back when John the friendly local postman brought her a longish parcel, which she was anxiously expecting, to the front door of her little house next to the church.

With heart thumping, she locked the front door and opened the parcel on her big double bed. The jet-black and shiny dildo was alarmingly more than 30 cm. It was as thick and round as a street gangster's baton.

Twisting a knob at the bottom end of it brought it alive and it vibrated on the mattress. It was Monday morning and Mary had a whole list of things to do, but she had to try the instrument immediately.

The previous night, Mary had a very vivid wet dream so real that it gave her an almighty orgasm that woke her up sweating and panting.

She had fallen asleep after masturbating with her fingers while watching a short and very realizing porn clip showing the large bottom of an English housewife being fucked by a black African's huge and long dong.

She could see that the poor woman was really struggling to contain the size of the man in her anus, and the outsized tool was really causing her both pain and pleasure at the same time.

As the housewife was yelling her house down, so was Mary as she reached an orgasm so intense that she almost fainted, and probably did briefly, for all she knew.

As if that Internet fucking was not enough. In her wet dream that followed, Mary was similarly mounted in the bum hole by a sweaty black plantation slave, who was packed solid with muscles, including the long black one that was decimating her anus all night.

Mary was wearing one of the long beautiful dresses of Scarlet O'Hara in Gone with the Wind.

She was cornered at the back of the cotton slave quarters and bent over and well and truly fucked with the back of her pretty dress pushed over her head to expose her white soft bottom to the mercy of the black man.

If he had any mercy, he was not showing it, and Clark Gable was nowhere to be found to barge in to rescue her. But she actually did not want to be rescued.

Mary now puts some hand oil she has on the dildo. Then, like Scarlet, she kneels on the carpet and bends over the edge of the bed, flipping her skirt over her back.

Should postman come now and look in the window to the bedroom, he would see the village pastor's round and full behind, pointing invitingly at him.

With her eyes closed, and thinking of

bank manager Samuel, Mary reached back to slowly insert the blunt bullet head of the black dildo into her anus.

With initial resistance from her anus, the machine slips in fairly comfortably. When it is turned on, Mary can hardly stand the sensation. Again for her, Samuel is behind, pushing his big prick in and sending her forehead banging on the mattress.

The trusty dildo is now kept permanently under the other pillow on her bed and is used very often by the pastor.

In her thoughts almost constantly now, Mary works out how she can fuck Samuel.

The odds of course are stacked against her. A preacher trying to seduce a member of the flock away from his wife? Certainly it's a scenario drafted by Mephistopheles himself to enjoy.

Last Sunday, Mary took care to shake Samuel's hand warmly after church and looked deeply into his gorgeous eyes. She took care to ask him and his wife how they were settling in.

She saw that Samuel noticed the special attention, and that he left quite puzzled.

Going back to church later to close it up for the day, Mary is surprised to see Samuel on one of the back pews, deep in contemplation. Her heart is thumping as she approaches him.

"Hi Pastor," he says with his charming smile.

By God, this man is handsome, thinks Mary.

"I was just taking time to say a prayer

before dinner," he says. "Have you eaten?"

"No, I am just closing up then I'll fix myself something simple," says Mary and adds quickly, "Would you like to share a beer with me? It would be a nice change from drinking by myself."

"I'd love too, thanks, Pastor. Got a bit of time," he says.

Mary is pouring the beer in the kitchen when Samuel suddenly comes to stand close behind her and presses his crotch against her bottom.

Then he hugs her around the waist.

"Samuel!" says Mary quietly, very surprised.

"Please don't be alarmed," says the parishioner, as he lifts Mary's skirt up from the back.

"I'm not," says Mary.

"Whoa!" he says, as it's his turn to be surprised to see the preacher's bare ass, since Mary often goes around without underwear to feel more sensual.

The pastor spills some beer as Samuel grabs her now between her legs. The pastor is melting with pleasure already.

"Not here please, Samuel," quietly says Mary. "Follow me."

In her bedroom, at roughly the masturbation spot on the bed in her bedroom, Mary's wet dream is becoming alarmingly real.

Just like in the dream, the pastor now kneels down and bends over on one side of the bed. She has stripped entirely, and now her large round behind is waiting.

Then, as in the dream, it's Samuel this time who is the African whose huge penis is spearing into her body.

Never in her experience has her poor cunt had to try to accommodate anything so large and long. It's as if Samuel is dangling another of her black dildo between his legs.

Not only satisfied with her tight vagina, once lubricated with the creative moisture from inside there, the black rod seeks to finish inside her anus.

But that is not an easy task. Mary enjoys anal sex, if only with her black dildo in recent years. But she is defending against this intruder now that is forcing its way into the wrong passage.

"Jesus Christ, oh sweet Jesus!" she blasphemes. "I'm being split apart. Easy, dearest Samuel."

"Don't worry, Pastor," says Samuel, "We're almost there." And they are.

The explosions of her orgasms are what Mary enjoys most about sex, but this one is a nuclear blast. Her whole house is probably trembling, while their chorus of loud noises is reverberating in it. Good thing there are no neighbors within earshot.

"Holy Moses!" pants the banker, as he collapses on top of Mary's poor ass, pushing his dong even deeper.

"I've got to get back. Judy has my dinner in the oven," says Samuel, smiling.

After church service the following Sunday, Mary, as usual, stands at the church door to shake hands and chat to her congregation.

As she delivers her sermon, the church congregation notices a bloom on the face of their female pastor, and some of the men sense her beauty and sexuality for the first time.

Toward the back, Samuel certainly does notice the difference.

Samuel and his wife warmly shake her hand, and Mary even embraces Judy.

It's a warm night when Mary goes to close up the church. Samuel is at his usual place on the pew where they first met.

They embrace rather fiercely, grabbing each other hard, needing to satisfy a hunger that has built up during the working week.

Mary breaks away with difficulty and beckons Samuel with her index finger to follow her, picking up a small blanket along the way.

The night is dark and overcast as the lovers make their way between the headstones in the cemetery at the back to an old oak tree in the corner of the plot.

There the pastor slowly undresses the favorite member of her flock, neatly folding his jacket and shirts on an old stone slab of a grave.

When she frees Samuel's prized penis from his briefs and lets it hang loose, Mary can't resist fondling and feeling the latent and heavy muscular strength of it.

Normally, not liking to put men's penises

in her mouth, wary of where those things may have been, Mary now licks the formidable shiny black head of Samuel's perfect specimen.

The man groans as his weapon levers up alarmingly in immediate response, ever ready to go into the next battle. He helps Mary to undress and buries his nose and face into the ample bushiness of her cunt.

Mary spreads the blanket on a black marble slab of a new grave of a young girl, she believes, who died mysteriously recently.

Then she lays down on it facing up and spreading her legs apart, reliving yet another of her vivid nightly fantasies.

Samuel loses no time to kneel between her thighs, and he separates a little more to fit down on his knees.

Mary now pulls out from her bag next to her what looks like a horrible crumpled head.

"Oh, God! What the hell is that?" whispers Samuel.

"Not God, but the other," says Mary. "It's a mask of Him. Can you put it on?"

"Oh, kinky, Pastor." laughs the towering black man.

The floppy rubber mask is ghastly in its realism. It's complete with pointy red horns that wobble about. The face of the Devil has an awful leering grimace in the rubber folds of its dark facial skin.

If Samuel were to walk about on such a night abroad from the cemetery now, he would frighten the life out of anyone in the village.

As it is, from where Mary is laying, horrible Mephistopheles has definitely come for a visit from hell.

There is a sharp pang where his iron rod of a penis misses its mark of her hole and barges into Mary's clitoris.

"Oh, fuck!" yells Mary, softly, surprised at her own language.

"Now, now, Pastor! Language, language," laughs Samuel. "What would your congregation say?"

"Fuck the congregation," laughs Mary. "But I also command you to fuck me now, Lucifer. I can't wait any more."

"With extreme pleasure," groans Samuel. Mary feels the Devil's long and thick tail slipping in.

Again, as a theologian, Mary has always wondered why the wonders of sex have been attributed only to the Devil, who must be a happy and sated being all the time, with millions of people on earth fornicating in his honor every single day and night.

Lying on her back in a cemetery, Mary feels part of the history of her village and congregation. What lives did the dead here have?

The horrible Devil on top of her and between her legs is growling now. Samuel is no longer the town's banker or her lover, but a large, dark being that has materialized out of the impending storm.

As he growls some more, Mary hears footsteps running away from behind the thick bushes and the stone wall of the cemetery to her left.

Young lovers? She wonders how long they had been there spying.

But then how would they tell anyone that they had seen no less than the Devil fucking their pastor in the village cemetery that night of the approaching storm.

17 LESBIAN'S RETREAT

Jodie and Jess have been friends since they were tottering around in kindergarten, and are more like sisters really.

Tonight is the usual Saturday night for them, out with Mark and Joachim, their latest boyfriends. As usual, the boys play pool with their buddies and their girlfriends of the tight and faded denim brigade, gossip and watch music videos on the TV on the wall.

Then the four hit the hamburger place, driving in Joachim's parents' rather swanky new white Chevrolet. Not knowing where else to go in this little town, like in Don Mclean's American Pie, they head for the levee, the town's water reservoir, which isn't dry, like in the hit song.

There they find their usual recent parking

place off the road, under a spreading elm and behind some bushes. A half moon is rising on the other side of the big lake and pairs of the town's lovers, at least in two other cars hidden in the forest at some distance, are also enjoying their usual Saturday night's freedom.

"Let's fuck, man," announces Mark to Joachim, and not particularly to the girls. "You had Jess last time, so let's swap and you grab Jodie?

"Is that OK with you girls?"

"It's OK with us girls," says Jess. "Fucking one of you is the same as fucking the other or any other boys around, isn't it Jodie?"

"Sure," says Jodie.

"That's nice!" says Joachim. "Did you hear that, Mark?"

"Whatever, man," says Mark. "Whatever they say, I like fucking whichever one of these two. Which have I got tonight again?"

"Me," says Jodie, who happens to be sitting on the back seat beside Mark already. The young man immediately starts to feel Jodie's breasts clumsily, and then he unbuttons her blouse.

On the front seat, Joachim is fumbling with his fly, as he leans back on the passenger side to slip down his pants, while Jess climbs astride him, and peels off her tight T-shirt to let her delectable boobs swing free.

"Good God," says Joachim, as his mouth reaches for either of the available pink nipple that is in reach.

Jodie in the back lays back, half naked, to actually enjoy Mark's clumsy exploration of her body. The man's hand is between her big thighs, seeing what its fingers can find down there in the moist groove.

Clumsy or not, Jodie lets herself feel all his movement, allowing this pampering that should lead soon to bigger things.

In front of her is the lovely face of her lifelong friend, already transported with her eyes half-shut and her sweet mouth falling open.

"Wait," whispers Jodie. Jess nods.

Finally Jodie is all bare, laying back at full stretch on her back in the spacious car. Without much foreplay, Mark's dork is already inside her, slipping in and out pleasurably but also mechanically.

The two young women are looking each other, as they sometimes do in their joint masturbation sessions. They smile at each other now, with some difficulty, as their individual climaxes approach.

The boys in the meantime are yelling and grunting away, as was their wont, when their turns come, shaking the new car like a ship riding big waves.

Jess and Jodie reach for each other's hands and let their joint shuddering orgasms take them away from this routine Saturday night scene for some brief moments.

The two women only recently started to masturbate together.

The first time was quite memorable. The close friends were spending the night in Jess's apartment at the back of her parents' suburban house, as they often did over the years.

It was actually Jess's birthday, and her parents invited friends and family for a happy party.

Jess and Jodie were tipsy from many glasses of good wine as the two tottered back to Jess's room for the night, their arms draped over each other's shoulder and waist.

Tired, undressed and crashed, naked and drunk, on the two single beds on opposite sides of Jess's bedroom.

In all the years of their friendship, this is the first time that they had seen each other naked. And they liked what they saw.

"Don't know about you, Jodie, but I'm pretty horny," said Jess, who had flopped on her front on the top of her bed, exposing her lovely firm round peach-like bottom to the ceiling.

She flipped over now, the pale nipples on her full breasts standing upright, and her golden hair forming an exciting stuff on her small pubic mound.

"Don't look, but I usually fuck myself to sleep," said Jess, her words slurring.

"I'll join you," said Jodie, spreading her

legs now luxuriously on her bed, enjoying the freedom of being bare.

She also enjoyed seeing Jess there with her thighs open, with her fingers slowly rubbing the gash of her cunt.

"Wait for me, and we'll come together?" said Jodie.

"OK, but hurry. Am almost there," said Jess, her knees now stuck up with both feet are held up in the air for the final assault.

"Fucking hell, fucking hell," she screamed while Jodie was also wracked by an overwhelming onslaught, that also tossed her body about.

The girlfriends have recently preferred these mutual erotic sessions by themselves to fucking the boys, who have drifted off to other girls in the meantime.

While enjoying different ways to come in each other's company, the girls have strangely hesitated to touch each other, perhaps in the same way that sisters don't do so.

The closest they came to touching was one night when they shared the lounge in Jodie's place while each was masturbating to a particularly erotic movie about lesbian love that Jodie had borrowed for the night.

The two had their thighs opened facing each other on the small lounge, their knees were touching.

The full views of their vulvas gaping wide, along with the sensual aroma floating up from them, sent the women off early to their destinations.

"You know we should look up Camille," says Jess, referring to just about the only lesbian friend that they knew at school. "Wonder what she is up to now? Bet she can show us a few nice tricks."

"Do you want to be lesbians together?" asks Jess.

"Yes let's," says Jodie.

"Yeah, let's invite her to my parents' place in the mountain," said Jess, "and we can have a weekend lesbian retreat."

"Brilliant idea, Jess," says Jodie.

Their anticipated first lesbian days came very quickly. The three women are in Jodie's station wagon heading for the mountains, on the road made more glorious by autumnal hues of the forests on either side.

Jodie's parents were more than happy that the three friends were taking their retreat in this marvelous time of early fall.

The parents were in fact half-hinting that they would like to come too but then luckily worried about crowding the girls. And they would have in more ways than one.

Sitting in the back of the car, Camille has bloomed into a very pretty young woman, with beautiful long auburn hair.

Like Jodie, she is a graphic designer and loves her free and easy life with a casual string of lesbian encounters.

Intrigued by the weekend project of the lesbians-to-be, Camille readily agreed to be their teacher, especially when her old school friends have become very attractive women.

The mountain chalet is an ideal one for a retreat, set into a hillside in a thick pine forest, miles from another weekend house.

A large balcony looks over the trees over to the lake and the low mountains around it. There is a big wooden tub Jacuzzi to one side of it.

The women take their bags upstairs to the master bedroom and decide to sleep together in the big bed there.

"Can I lay down a couple of weekend rules?" asks Camille, draping her arms over her two willing lesbian students.

"One: no clothes whatsoever the entire weekend. Two: as many orgasms as are physically possible!" she says. "Starting now!"

The women strip with abandon and soon are gloriously bare. They try awkward steps, dancing their new freedom to music from the hi-fi against the vista of forests and mountains.

"Let's Jacuzzi," invites Jodie.

The girls are soon relaxed in the hot

bubbling bath, admiring the evening sunset through the trees and catching the last rays on the lake.

"We conveniently have three water spouts of this thing, so we can take one each and open our legs to them and let the jets do their work," directs Camille.

"But first we should hug and kiss each other. Not just pecks on the lips, but fat wet kisses that we used to give to the boys," she says. "Like this."

Camille gently hugs Jodie and kisses her, while her hands sensuously feel both of Jodie's breasts. Then an expert hand moves down to feel Jodie's cunt for the first time.

Jodie savors those first touches, as she opens her thighs now to the strong jet of warm water.

Camille in the meantime is deep into her first hug of Jess, taking her time to feel the shape of Jess's lovely bottom, touching the tight pucker of her anus, then following the valley further down.

The girls now abandon themselves to the will of the water jets, letting the force of the water open the petals of their flowers under water.

They can feel the jets trying to push into their vaginas, and enjoy their slightly-too-firm massage of their clitorises.

Underwater hands are also caressing unidentified thighs, breasts and bottoms, as the three ladies are straining for their first orgasms for the weekend.

With hair soaked and faces half submerged, the three close their eyes to feel the bubbling waves and their own mini-tsunamis rearing up between their legs.

Jess is first to arch up out of the waves to expose her full and perfectly-shaped breasts, before falling back into the bath with a fierce cry.

Jodie is next, pressing her forehead to the rim of the wooden tub, while both hands are grabbing that rim. Half of her face is submerged and her incomprehensible words are bubbling underwater.

"That ... is ...excellent, girls ...," says teacher Camille, with some difficulty, as she herself is threshing around under water by her own orgasm.

"Wow!," says Jess, who spontaneously kisses Jodie full on the mouth for the first time, in some kind of gratitude, maybe for her parents' place, or for the weekend.

Teacher Camille looks on with approval.

"Nicely done, girls," she says. "One down and many to go?"

The girls had great time cooking pasta for dinner, feeling strange and exhilarated with everyone in the nude. Cooking and also eating the meal in the nude should be done more often, they agreed.

After dinner and many glasses of red wine, the girls light a roaring fire in the fireplace and fill the comfortable lounge with the sweet smell of pine wood.

In a scene which reminds the two graphic artists of paintings by Balthus that depict naked young girls by a fire place, the girls spread themselves around on the thick carpet letting their limbs toast in the radiant heat from the fire.

Like Balthus girls, the three amuse themselves by crawling around on all fours, to show off their lovely bottoms to each other. They dance and skip to ballet music playing on the hi-fi.

For Camille, it's a rather overwhelming feast of female beauty, as naked Jess and Jodie are simply divine.

Camille pushes the comfy lounge closer to the front of the fire. Pouring more red wine into their glasses, the girls sit together on the lounge and begin to caress each other, led by Camille.

The teacher's hands are gently everywhere, feeling here, rubbing there, kneading and spreading.

Amazingly Jess and Jodie have put aside their reticence about touching each other and are embracing with arms and legs entwined.

"We won't have anything to do with men this weekend, so we won't use a dildo that is after all a mechanical penis," says Camille. "We'll just use our fingers."

Jess now finds herself the center of the action. She is leaning back against the spread out thighs of Camille whose strong hands are squeezing her breasts, then firmly cupping her open cunt.

Then naughty Jodie gets in on the act

and is poking her fingers everywhere between Jess' legs.

At one stage, smiling Jodie has her index finger in Jess' vagina, sliding it in and out like a little penis, while Camille's index finger is rubbing Jess's clitoris at the same time, sending her crazy.

Now that Jodie is kissing her again on her mouth very pleasantly and sexily.

Jess can't hold on any more and was off, pushing up her cunt and arching her back, and screaming blue murder.

Camille lets Jess gyrate away to her satisfaction, and letting herself also come more quietly from the repeated impact of Jess' bottom on her cunt.

Jodie's turn comes next. Jess, still shaking from her own orgasm, now climbs astride Jodie and presses her vulva into Jodie's face and mouth.

Camille in the meantime has slipped down on to the carpet and is at work with her expert mouth on Jodie's genitals.

For lucky Jodie then, this is a unique and overwhelming experience that she wishes can last all night. She has never felt anything like Camille's snake-like tongue that is darting in and out everywhere.

At the same time Jodie is trying the same on Jess's cunt that is pressing and rubbing hard on her nose and mouth, as Jess is approaching yet another of her climaxes.

Consciously abandoning herself completely, Jodie is also arriving fast, her whole body being gripped by a tense muscular force from somewhere.

The poor lounge is thumping on the carpet as Jess and Jodie again achieve simultaneous orgasms.

"You are getting good girls!" says Camille. "I am very impressed."

"I'm heading for bed now but before I sleep, can I give you both the task of making me come. Do you think you can do that?"

The women are interrupted by men's voices outside.

Alarmed, Jodie quickly turns the lights off, so that the room is lit only by light from the fire.

The women crawl over to peek behind the drawn curtains, where three bare bottoms are pointing back.

Three burly men, armed with big hunting rifles, are at the gate of the house, looking at Jodie's car, and up to their window.

"I think I saw three women driving past on the highway this afternoon," says one of the men. "Shall we go and pay them a visit? They did look spunky."

"Naw, leave them be. Let's hunt deer, not loose women, or lesbians," says another. The men walk on, laughing.

"Phew, I thought we had a problem then," says Camille. "Men are always a problem."

Teacher Camille herself has never has such a night as this one. She is comfortable and warm in bed. On either side of her are the soft flesh of two new lesbians whose hands are everywhere pleasurably on her body.

She turns around to kiss one and the other is waiting for her kiss also on the other side.

These students of hers are so insistent and they learn so well that teacher doesn't have to do much but enjoy their manipulation. To help bring on one memorable orgasm for Camille late into the night, Jess' finger was in her anus; Jodie's was in her vagina while Camille's finger was at work on her clitoris.

For the three lesbian sisters, there really needs to be no end to this retreat that can continue when they return home.

18 MEXICAN HITCHHIKER

"I am, how you say, two sex," says the Mexican hitchhiker in broken English, thick with a tuneful Spanish accent, from the backseat.

"You mean bisexual. Good for you," says Megan in her surprise. She exchanged smiles with her boyfriend Bruce who was driving.

"My name is Anton. I come from Mexico, to go fruit picking in the USA," says their passenger.

Illegal immigrant or not, he stands stripped of his clothes just now in Megan's imagination, his body tanned and rippling with muscles—almost the opposite of the gentle flabbiness of her Bruce.

"Stop! I want to pick up that one," yells Megan, after their car had sped past Anton, standing in the blazing sun by the side of the long stretch of empty highway stretching out through the vast desert.

"Wow, a spunky one. I wouldn't mind him between my legs in the sack!" says Megan, as they wait for the man to run to the car. "Would you mind that?"

"... Er, I guess not, dearest," says Bruce, who always aims to please her.

"We are going camping at the Grand Canyon for the weekend," says Megan to Anton in the back of the car. "We would love you to come with us. We have a tent big enough for three people. Have you seen the Grand Canyon? It must be one of the seven wonders of the world."

"I start work in Las Vegas now," says Anton.

"Oh please!" says Megan, rather desperate now. We'll drop you at work in Vegas on Monday."

"OK," says the Mexican, himself already feeling clearly Megan's sex appeal.

"I massage your shoulder while we drive?" Ramon asks, reaching forward to place his strong hands on her shoulders.

"Oh, OK!" says Megan, surprised again. "What service!"

Bruce too raises his eyebrows.

Megan leans back and feels the strength of the fingers, which would be devastating on other parts of her body. After a long while, she asks Bruce to stop to let her get into the back for Ramon to massage her easier.

Again, Bruce aims to please her.

Ramon has leaned back against one door and opens his blue-jeaned legs for Megan to present her back to him. He continues to massage her back.

Megan soon kind of swoons back to rest on the solid muscles of Ramon's chest with her eyes closed, in dreamland.

Ramon's amazing hands have now come under her arms to cup both of her soft full breasts.

"Wow," whispers the woman.

"Are you OK?" asks Bruce from the front, not being able to see what is happening directly behind his seat.

"Great, Bruce, really great," moans Megan.

Megan feels that this man can probably bring her to orgasm, just by caressing and kneading her breasts and nipples in the way that he is doing now. But his right hand has slowly moved down to cup the crotch of her tight jeans, which her legs have conveniently opened for him.

As he squeezes her cunt, Megan can feel that hand and opens up for it as if the thick jeans are not there.

But Ramon has read her thoughts and his fingers undo the top of her jeans and now push their way deliciously down to her open cunt.

"Oh, Jesus, don't stop," whispers Megan in Ramon's ear. He smiles.

Megan feels a strong thick middle finger sliding slowly down her crack that is well wet by now, caressing her clitoris and sending a shudder through her whole being.

Just when Megan can't hold on any longer, the finger suddenly curls up and slips up the tight hole of her vagina.

That is then, the final straw, as Megan hopelessly tries to contain her orgasm. She tenses up to manage her shuddering that is rocking the car and also bites her tongue so as not to scream and startle the driver.

"Everything OK," asks Bruce rather anxiously now from the front, craning to look back in the rear-vision mirror.

"...Good... Bruce," manages Megan, who has collapsed back into the welcoming body of Ramon. "Fantastic massage, back here."

It's eerily quiet at the Grand Canyon. Every time that Megan comes here, this is the first thing noticeable there. It is as if all the sound in the world has fallen into the vast chasm of the ancient canyon.

Always present also is the spiritual space that sustained the Hopi Indians for centuries.

Megan and Bruce have their favorite camping place, well away from the tourist village and tour-bus stopping places. It's tucked away at the end of the camping site, close to cliff edge and the sheer long drop into the canyon.

They set up their tent and cook a meal on the gas stove in the open, then watch the brilliant spectacle of a blood-red sunset, washed down by cans of beer.

In the warm and beautiful twilight, by the light of the camp fire, Megan simply decides to take her clothes off, as the men watch.

She knows the effect of her spectacular body on men, and she can see that both men are absorbed in the view, even Bruce who knows her body all too well by now.

She sits down on a patch of grass and says, "Your turn now, guys."

Hesitating, Bruce stands up and starts to strip. Megan always enjoys the feminine appearance of Bruce's body, with its pale skin and softer curves.

It's bare now. His long thin penis hangs down from a thick blond tuff of curly hair.

"Bravo!" says Ramon, enjoying the sight also.

"Your turn, Mexican boy," orders Megan in anticipation. She is not disappointed.

Here is the body of a real he-man, the Marlboro man riding into the desert sunset, the likes of which she has never seen, not in such glorious male flesh right there in front of her.

The fire light dramatically bathes the body, highlighting the bulges of his muscular chest, his thighs, and the large muscular penis growing out of its jet-black bush.

This vision of pure maleness gives Megan an ache in her groin.

"Fancy tucking in early, boys?" asks Megan. "You guys make me horny!"

"Horny?" asks Ramon. "What is horny?"

"Me! That's what horny is," says Megan, laughing. "Horny means you want to fuck."

"Oh, fuck. Yes, I want fuck," says Ramon.

"Well, come on then, big boy. Just look at you, would you?" says Megan, marveling at the angry-looking thick penis pointing at her face.

"Come on, Brucie," says Megan. "To work in the tent, boys."

Bruce has never seen Megan so full of passion; as soon as the three crawled into the tight-fitting tent, practically ignoring him, she opens her welcoming thighs to Ramon, who plows in ahead, like a bull into the bullfight arena.

The two struggling bodies, working up a real sweat by now, are right next to him in the crowded space. Ramon is mechanically working up a storm, and clearly his Megan is swept up into it.

"Oh fuck, oh fuck," she says repeatedly, moving and yielding to the galloping Mexican on top of her. Bruce is fascinated by the big penis as Ramon thrusts it into Megan's tight opening, accompanied by a sloshing sound, while the tent is filled with the strong smell of sex.

Again, in all his time with her, Bruce has

never seen his lover quite this excited. At their peak, the two lovers threaten to blow up the inflatable air mattress underneath them all.

Then, Megan raises the tent's dome roof with her screaming that floats out into the silent canyon.

"Your turn, Brucie," pants Megan, somewhat devastated by this Mexican charging bull. The man himself has withdrawn to make room for Bruce.

What a performance to have to follow, thinks Bruce, but he is so worked up by what he has just seen that Megan's open cunt, still wet, is what he now must have.

Megan has opened her legs wider and has completely abandoned herself to this incredible double camping treat. With good old Bruce huffing away on top of her, Megan looks at dear Ramon, resting beside her.

Even familiar Bruce has somehow gained some staying power and is still slogging away pleasurably to his usual shaking orgasm.

As the three bodies are collapsed and entwined on each other, the peaceful night returns. Megan hears furtive footsteps among the trees outside. Other campers, the park ranger, or animals? Who cares.

Megan wakes again towards the morning. To her surprise, her Brucie is crouching on his knees, waiting for Ramon who has his hard prick poised on Bruce's anus.

"Whoah, Brucie," says Megan. "What's come over you?"

"I tell him, try fucking a man, me!" says a smiling Ramon, as his big dick slips into Bruce's bottom.

"Good God," screams Bruce. "It's excruciating!"

"Feel good for me," says Ramon.

"And me," giggles Megan, who has never seen anal fucking by men in the flesh, and certainly not at such close range.

Somewhat worn out by their nocturnal excesses, the campers take an easy day sightseeing and sitting for hours in the shade of pine trees right at the edge of the vast silent chasm.

Packing up their camp, they descend on the long steep tracks, zigzagging down to the bottom of the canyon where water roars by in a big cool river.

They crane their necks to look up perpendicular brown and gold sides of the formidable canyon, having stepped down through millions of years of geological history.

Towards the evening, again the three discarded their clothes, going back in time themselves to the centuries when the Hopi Indians lived here, and even to an earlier time of the early humans, maybe living in caves around there.

"Let us be naked and sleep in a cave tonight," says Megan. "And we live like the Indians for a while."

The cave they found is large within view of the river. There are faint markings on the walls from earlier habitation.

For the men, the glorious sight of Megan naked is a real joy. Bruce, who knows his partner's body well, is rapt seeing it in broad daylight, walking about freely.

There is no doubt about it; this vision of the woman is full of sex appeal: her large haunches invite invasion, and her perfect white breasts and full stomach call to be grabbed and laid upon.

And the perfect triangle of blond pubic hair that barely hides the mesmerizing opening in the middle of the growth.

In the cool of the summer evening, Megan announces:

"Hey guys, I feel horny again. So give me half an hour to go to hide in this forest around here. And the one who can find me can fuck me good."

She puts on her walking boots and the men see her inviting bottom disappearing into the forest. The would-be hunters wait their turn impatiently.

Sunlight recedes quickly from the bottom of this deep valley. Megan soon realizes that she is lost and is trying to follow the sound of the river back to it. All the while, she is looking out for someone who may pounce on her from behind a bush or a tree.

Near another set of hollows in the sandstone cliff, Megan hears movement.

She crouches on her knees on the grass behind some bushes, feeling very exposed in her bottom, just when something heavy falls right on it.

In the gloom, a muscular body has mounted her from behind and grabbed her torso and breasts and her long hair quite hard so she can't turn around to see which of the men it is.

From the feel of the hard muscles, in the tight embrace of which she can hardly move, Megan thinks that it must be Ramon. But the man has a different sweaty feel and smell.

And when the assaulter's hard thick penis penetrates her, Megan knows that it is not Ramon. She struggles now in vain to turn around to see who it is. She thinks, her long black hair in braids swinging.

"Whoever this guy is, he has stamina," thinks Megan. Despite being forced and rather painfully held by her hair, the woman is wanting the attack to continue.

The extra hard and muscular intruding cock is soon sending Megan off, as her head bangs the grass, and she finds herself making strange Indian attacking noises that she remembers from cowboy films.

Even when she is finished and panting, the man on her back is still going until he too quietly shoves and jerks in final finishing movements.

Then before Megan can turn around to see more of him, the ghostly attacker has vanished into the darkness.

"Jesus. What was that?" mumbles the woman to herself, as she recovers from the onslaught.

She still is not sure where she is, and the night is growing darker. She may have to spend a cold night in the forest here. Stumbling on a few paces, Megan gives up the idea as her bare body is scratched by sharp dead branches.

Still there is no sign of her two men.

As Megan lies down and gathers leaves and pine needles, she is pushed down onto the soft carpet of leaves from behind.

Again, before she can see who, the shadowy muscular figure pins her to the ground by his sheer weight.

As Megan screams, an iron of a palm grabs her hard and painfully around her mouth until she struggles to breathe.

This attacker is shorter and stockier than the first one and has muscles of steel. Again she can't turn around to see the dark and illusive figure.

Then, there is a sharp pain as the attacker's iron penis forces itself into her anus.

Megan screams into the muffling palm grip around her mouth and feels as if she has been stabbed in that sensitive place.

Again, despite the helplessness of being overcome, the woman can let herself feel the firm movement of the cock as it slides in deeply, then pulls out, then barges in again.

Despite the muscle in her bottom trying to expel the intrusion, she is also nevertheless enjoying the size and length of the rock-hard penis.

Despite not wanting to reward the attack with any satisfaction, Megan can't hold back another orgasm, which explodes in her bottom, in a way that she has never felt before.

Again, like the first attacker, this man gallops on without slowing, well after sending Megan crumbling into the ground.

This time the woman takes advantage of that stamina and allows herself another climax, as overwhelming as the first, or even more so.

When Megan recovers and opens her eyes again, the second ghostly rapist has melted back into the darkness of the night.

Searching frantically by torch light now, Bruce and Anton come upon Megan, laying on her front, her body dusty and scratched.

They take her down to the river and go into the cool water with her to clean her up.

Then, the three lay down on a mattress of grass and blanket, the men on either side, cuddling their precious and exhausted Megan.

19 AN ABORIGINAL LOVER

Paul only vaguely remembered the après-ski party – it was more of an orgy, really. Everyone in their university ski group was very merry and very drunk when they struggled back from the Aspen bar through the thick snow and the mini-blizzard that was blowing in their faces.

Fueled by plenty of Glühwein and Schnapps guzzled in front of a roaring fire, the students had paired up and lost no time at all in tumbling down into bunks, onto the sofa and the thick carpet in their large cabin.

Someone built up the fire that poured heat into the room. Ski boots, woolen hats and thick gloves went flying off first. The feisty girls were first to strip, some teasing the boys by swinging their tops, bras and underpants over their heads, much to the loud cheering of the men.

For Paul, it was somewhat unreal to see the inhibition of some of the quiet, nice girls he knew from class melt away in the warm cabin. Spectacular white and pink bodies were quickly liberated from the cover of lots of clothing.

Some amazingly shapely bodies were revealed and flaunted. Full breasts jiggled and bounced; curly blond and red pubic triangles glinted in the fire light, accompanied by much giggling.

The muscular men, too, bared their young, sportive bodies, as if following a signal by someone to suddenly turn the party into a wild orgy.

To laughter and more muffled giggling, some couples, especially those in bunks that offered more privacy, quickly went at it, with exposed white male muscular bottoms plowing away among the beddings.

One couple had the honor of being first to reach their long and noisy orgasms, which put broad grins on the faces of other couples who were grabbing and exploring each other's bodies.

Paul was still without a partner, but he saw that his friend, Jane, was sitting by herself, overwhelmed by the scene.

He was just about to move to her when he noticed Jinny, the Australian Aboriginal exchange student, sitting in a corner sofa, smiling at the goings-on. He went to her instead, avoiding Jane's gaze.

"Hi," he said, smiling. "It's getting a bit

hot and noisy in here, isn't it, Jinny?"

"Yeah," she nodded with a smile, her perfect teeth white against the dark skin of her beautiful face. "They are not wasting much time," she said, still smiling. The slim, lanky girl signaled for Paul to sit next to her.

"Let's not waste our time, either," she said, grabbing Paul's hand. "I haven't had a decent screw since I left 'ome. So fuck me?"

Paul obliged by clumsily feeling for her breasts, then hugging her awkwardly. They kissed, again clumsily.

"Sit on top of me," Jinny directed him.

As Paul straddled her, Jinny quickly pulled down his ski pants; his underwear went with them. She then leaned back on the plush sofa and pulled his thick, pink cock toward her mouth.

The couple on the lounge next to them was setting the world on fire, the plump blond girl galloping away on top as if there was a race to be won. Her tremendous squeaking crescendo came first, accompanied by a lot of swearing; then it was her partner's turn to thrust his pelvis upward with a forceful grunt. They collapsed together, noisily.

Paul was sliding his penis into Jinny's mouth, while she sucked hungrily on it. He had pushed Jinny's head back to the sofa and was using the hole of her accommodating mouth like an open vagina.

He combed his hands through her lovely, curly, dark hair. When he could not hold back any longer, a warm, mountain stream released into Jinny's mouth and trailed down her throat.

Jinny gulped it all down with some noise then licked his cock clean.

"Yum," she said, with a broad smile. "I needed that!"

"Wow. Thank you, Jinny," said Paul. "Wow."

Later when things had died down a bit in the cabin, the two lovers found themselves curled up in a top bunk, both bare and warm together under the down bed covering.

They listened to another couple still in the middle of their muffled struggle somewhere close by in the dark, creaking the furniture. Lovers on the other bunks in the dark room were still.

Everything had calmed down, including the weather. The blizzard had blown away, leaving a pristine snowy wonderland lit by the few lights of the resort village.

Jinny was lying on her stomach, admiring the scene, and Paul found himself lying on top of her with his penis comfortable and warm in the valley of her bum. But the cock was stirring and firming up again.

"Hey, you are waking up down there, mate, I can feel it," whispered Jinny. "Fuck me in there, would you? Abo boys never do that, but I think it's very sexy."

Paul used his hand to probe the bulb of his cock into the opening of Jinny's vagina to lubricate it. Then he gently pressed the big tip of it inside her tight anus.

"Oh, fuck that would you? It feels so unreal!" murmured Jinny.

Paul felt his long penis easily slipping in to its full length as Jinny groaned some more. Her bum hole gripped his cock tightly, and he greatly desired to know its depths.

Paul slid his penis out slowly, almost to the tip, then slowly inched it back in again. He kissed the face of his lovely girl, half buried in the pillow, and his hand caressed her breasts and down to her cunt, combing through its short curls.

Jinny shuddered and wriggled gently.

"Oh, fucking hell. Oh, fuck," she whispered into the pillow.

Paul felt empowered by his control over her orgasm. He toyed with her for a while before allowing himself to join her in a long, full release.

"Oh, mate, I don't know how you bloody well did that," whispered Jinny, kissing him. "I never felt anything like that. I thought I was going to die. Promise me something? Come to see me in Australia, and do that to me again, all the bloody time?"

"I promise," laughed Paul, feeling as contented as he had ever been in his young life.

The Greyhound bus left a long plume of

bright-red dust as it sped down the road, straight as a spear thrown by Australian indigenous hunters at kangaroos or goanna lizards.

It was a long, straight road from Adelaide directly north to Alice Springs and the red heart of the vast Australian continent at Uluru.

Paul had not heard from Jinny since she flew off at the end of the semester; he had thought of her every day, and every night, since.

Their winter together was filled with days and nights the likes of which Paul had never known. Jinny had tired him out, in bed, in the shower, in the kitchen and the living room, whenever they had time in private together. They had made sure that they had plenty of that privacy at their disposal.

He had never met such a loving and affectionate girl, nor one with such incredible depth and mystery. He doubted that he would ever completely understand her, but he was willing to try.

But despite of all the mutual loving promises to keep in touch made when sweaty limbs and other organs were entwined, Paul had not received one letter or email from Jinny. No answers came from the email address that she gave him.

So after almost a year, Paul had saved enough money to buy a ticket to Australia.

Jinny said she lived near Uluru, the Aboriginal word for Ayer's Rock, a huge outcrop that was sacred to the Aborigines. It sat in the middle of a vast desert that glows red at sunrise and sunset each day.

But he had no address for her, and his trip was shaping to be a wild goose chase. What if she was married by now, or expecting a kid? What if she was away studying somewhere and was not home?

Paul didn't care. He had to try to see her, let come what may.

Before he boarded a bus to Uluru, Paul walked through town, backpack slung over his shoulder. He paused to ask some Aborigines who were trying to keep cool in the shade of big gum trees by the river if they knew of Jinny Watson. None of them had heard of her.

After another long dusty ride through the fascinating but seemingly endless desert of hot red sand, the bus pulled into the little township of Uluru, trailing a plume of dust.

The small town was there to serve the resorts and hotels that existed only to serve the plane-loads of tourists who came to pay their respect at dawn to Australia's red heart.

Paul checked into a room over the town's main pub. Then he headed straight to Tourist Information and was told that a Watson family lived at the edge of town at the end of the main street. He wasted no time.

With his heart pounding, and slightly out of breath, Paul stood at the fly-screen door of a fibro-house with a rusty iron roof. He knocked quietly.

It seemed like forever before a dark figure moved from the back door at the end of the corridor. The lovely face from so many of his dreams floated behind the fly-wire, wide-eyed.

"Paul? Bloody hell!" screeched Jinny as the rickety door flew open. She jumped up and wrapped her long, thin legs around him.

"How... How did you find me? I can't bloody believe this, I really can't!" Jinny cried with a broad smile.

"Not easy, Jinny. Especially if you disappear without trace into the desert for a whole year," smiled Paul.

"Sorry, mate. I've got my reasons. I'll tell you later," she shrugged. "Can't tell you how happy I am that you came, though. We've got a whole year of fucking to catch up with, starting now! Come on, what you waiting for?!"

It was all the encouragement Paul needed. They ducked into Jinny's dark bedroom and ripped off each other's clothing. They tumbled onto the bed, creaking springs.

Flipping Paul onto his back, Jinny marveled at the size and erectness of his white gum tree trunk, just as she slid down over it and began to rock her hips.

"I've forgotten how good you were down there," she moaned. As Jinny galloped on and rode Paul like a wild bronco, the whole flimsy house seemed to shake to its non-existent foundation in a cacophony of the rusty bed springs.

The sight of her lithe and sexy body, all open in front of him, was worth all the doubts and fears of the past twelve months.

Her orgasm was spectacular, as always, brewing from somewhere deep down between her shiny dark sweaty legs then bursting forth like firework.

"Dad is a policeman, but he won't be back a while," Jinny said later, as they lay in each other's arms on her small bed. The oven of a room, in which their copious sweat dripped and pooled, was a long way from their snowy love nest in Colorado.

"Let's go bush," she said, pushing herself up. "I'll grab our swag and we can take off. I know just the place. I'll leave dad a note, so that the whole of the town's police force won't come after us."

A small lake, billabong in Aboriginal language, rested amazingly in the middle of arid rock and sand and low scrubs of the vast desert, with Uluru towering above the near horizon.

All they had was a swag, a kind of a double sleeping bag, and some food.

"We can stay here a few days, but clothes are banned," Jinny said. "This is a nudist billabong! I come here to wander here naked, so now you can, too, if you want to stay."

"Whatever you say, my love," said Paul, surprised by the pet name he used. Jinny noticed, too.

Both stripped off the layers of the outside

world, glad to leave it behind for a few days.

As if to welcome them into the wild, a swarm of budgerigars, a mass of gold and green, wheeled down to drink at the water's edge, their noisy screeching deafening.

Leaping and dancing as the birds lifted off, Jinny's dark shiny body seemed to be a part of the spirit of the land.

She ran splashing into the cool water, diving in and showing a marvelous view of her bottom and the black hairy patch between her legs.

Paul dashed in, too, gasping as the unexpectedly cool water enveloped him.

When he surfaced he found that Jinny had swum to the other side of the lake and was wriggling up in the mud like a nubile young crocodile or python.

Then, glistening with mud and water, she crawled on all fours, pointing her round and inviting bottom in Paul's direction. She glanced back over her shoulder with a broad smile.

Paul, too, pretended that he was some kind of four-legged animal, maybe an albino wild boar that was charging up and grunting after a sow in heat.

In the slick mud the Paul animal mounted the Jinny animal and a muddy penis found its mark right away, piercing in. Patches of the afternoon sun dappled the muddy beach and from a distance, the grunting and squealing of the strange animal lovers somehow fit into the wild scene.

A whirling sound cut through the air

above them. A boomerang curled back above them to land by the bushes on one shore. Jinny started to yell in Aboriginal to the bushes on one side of the lake, laughing at the same time.

Laughter came back from some spying Aboriginal boys, who were well hidden in the bushes.

"Mad bastards," said Jinny with a smirk. "Don't mind them. They'll be off soon. A real nuisance they are." She yelled again at them.

That night all the stars in the night sky could be seen in the high, huge dome above. The naked lovers had climbed to the top of the Uluru Mountain, painfully, in their bare feet. They laid on their backs, spread eagle to the universe, tired and a little cold.

"Look at that, would you, Jinny?" sighed Paul. "How glorious."

"If you come over to fuck me now, the earth father will mate with the earth mother, and all will be well with the universe," said Jinny, smiling.

With his penis again well and securely inside its home within his Aboriginal girl, Paul let the doubts of the day float away.

Jinny still had her studies to finish, as did he, and it was all being done on opposite sides of the earth. Should he stay with her until she finished studying, then they could go home together?

Would she agree to come with him anyway, despite her studies, and leave this sacred universal rock of hers?

As usual, Paul loved to see his lover

working her way to yet another steep peak, as she had many times that incredible day. Again, she struggled and moved like an animal, undulating like a snake.

His penis felt like it was part of that movement, an earthly one, like the flow of larva or the mild tremble of an earthquake.

Climaxing, Jinny sang out some kind of chant that seemed to be coming from the rock on which they were fucking.

Jinny showed him a little hollow cave not far off where they took shelter for the night, sleeping on rocks that still held some heat from the blazing sun. From there, they would watch the sun rise on a new day and, Paul hoped, on their new life together.

20 HOME BOUND

Moira woke up suddenly in the middle of the night. The air moving through her suburban bungalow suggested that a window had been left open, but she was sure that she had shut them all before bed, one can never be too careful, especially at her more deserted end of the street.

Two dark shadows appear in her bedroom. Before she can make a sound, a strong hand is gently pressed to her mouth and other hands lightly gripped her arms.

"Not a sound, bitch, if you know what's good for you," says a gruff voice from the darkness. Another hulking man stuffs something that feels like a woman's stocking, probably her own, abruptly into her mouth, and ties it tightly behind her head while Moira made loud muffled sounds. She was steadily getting aroused.

"Don't make a sound, slut, no one will hear you," says the same hoarse voice. "We'll give it to you good if you don't stop it! We might do that anyway."

The other man tied her wrists to either side of the top of her bed so that she was effectively bound; she saw with some amusement that they were indeed using her very own stockings to bind her.

The gruff man with a shaven head tore apart her good short pajamas and then buried his mouth roughly on one nipple of her large bosom as soon as it is exposed.

The other man grasped the skimpy bottom of her flimsy panties and pulled them off her flailing legs. Moira felt his rough beard as he tried to put his mouth on her cunt, an action that made her breath begin to pick up and her pussy get wet from the sensation. There was not a need to gag and struggle against the bonds as she relaxed.

The intruders stood over the bottom of her big double bed and watched her naked form as she struggled helplessly to try to free her hands.

"Now, that's a sight for sore eyes, eh!" says Baldie. "Let me get at those big thighs and that big cunt."

The men each grabbed one leg and tied them to the end of the bed, leaving Moira spread-eagled.

"Now, that's much better, isn't it," says Beardie.

Easy Prize

The men surveyed their easy prize, taking their time to undress and then throw their clothes in a corner of the bedroom. Baldie tossed a coin into the air, caught it and slapped it on the back of the other hand.

"Head," says Beardie with a laugh. "Head it is."

"You've all the luck," says Baldie, shaking his head and pushing him.

"This is your lucky day, Bitch!" Beardie growled, as he crawled between Moira's legs and presses his mouth to her bushy vulva.

Moira wanted to struggle but then relaxed again as she felt the man's tongue and teeth roughly pressing into her before the heavy head worked its way along her full stomach onto her large breasts. The man rose above her as his thick hands kneaded both of her large tits, taking their time. Moira couldn't help enjoying the sensual kneading, her protests long forgotten. She began to moan at the new sensations she was feeling.

"Shut up, bitch!" he says. The same hands that fondled her breasts now are slapping them, causing some pain, but again also hidden pleasure at the same time.

There was a big cock poised on the gash of her pussy ready to penetrate her. It toyed with her for a moment, pressing in on her clitoris and then found her hole to barge in.

"How do you like that, bitch?" he growled at her. "There is plenty more of it so you better lay back and enjoy it, if you can.

The brute buried his face in her breasts again, as he finally shoved and jerked violently as he ejaculated.

Moira came as she felt him spill his seed inside her and the nipping at her breast with his teeth. She could only hope the next cock was as large as well as this one. She couldn't wait to have them both filling her at the same time.

Baldie's Turn

Baldie sat back on her dressing table chair, enjoying the scene that was reflected in her big dressing table mirror.

He stood, ready for his turn. "Let's turn her over," he said calmly while Beardie tied more pantyhose over Moira's mouth.

Her hands and ankles were untied, and the men flipped her over before quickly retying her again. Moira's heart pounded as her big bottom was exposed, leaving her totally at the men's mercy.

"Fuck, look at that ass, would you?" said Baldie. "Have you ever seen anything so big and sexy?"

"It is beautiful," agreed Beardie.

Moira had rarely felt the sensation that ripped through her as Baldie's hard cock poked into her asshole. Feeling the large dick inside her backside, forcing its way in and out, Moira follows its progress and braces herself for the for the final push that sends her over the edge, a silent orgasm careening through her. Then the weight of his whole body is on her back and his cock is still inside her. Perversely again, Moira enjoys being crushed like that into the mattress.

"She is some fuck, this slut," Baldie

gasped. "Wonder if she has any beer in the fridge. I've been starving too."

Helpless

Left to herself, all soiled and alone, with her bottom facing the ceiling, Moira wonders what is to come next. She can hear the clinking of bottles in the kitchen. In a while, the men are back, naked and hairy and looking all too pleased with themselves. Baldie has Moira's best big sharp kitchen knife. Beardie is carrying her big wooden spoon.

They put their cans of beer down. Baldie approached and sat on the bed, the knife now on the nightstand. Beardie came to sit on the opposite end with the wooden spoon in view.

Moira felt the spoon on her skin, poised in the middle of her back. Daring to move too much, she didn't struggle nor did he make a sound. She actually wondered what pleasure the men would bring her next.

"How are we going to do this, buddy?" asks Baldie.

"We haven't had our fill of her," Beardie replied.

"Maybe we slice her a bit where it hurts, just to wake her up," said Baldie.

Moira felt the point of the spoon moving slowly and precisely down her back, following the ridge of her spine. She doesn't think they would hurt her because there is no pain. The spoon moved to the top of the hill of her large ass and then went down the valley in the middle. Then the spoon traveled a little further down and rested on the soft entrance of her pussy.

Moira dared not move or even breathe. The spoon moved away altogether and immediately there was a sting on one cheek of her bottom, accompanied by a slapping sound. Moira screamed from the sharp pain as well as the surprise.

"Whack!" then the other cheek began stinging badly. "Whack!" the other fat bum cheek is hit again. Beardie was spanking her mercilessly with her big kitchen spoon.

"Now, are you going to behave?" he asked with a laugh. "We're going to cut you loose and untie your mouth. But if you as much as make a sound or try to run away, we'll tie you up again and slap you even harder. Understand?"

Moira nodded. This was the best part of her fantasy, bound, spanked and fucked.

House Slave

With her kitchen knife, the men cut her loose. After the men freed her mouth, Moira stood like a lost girl at the foot of the bed, in the front of the men, not saying a word.

"We're starving, bitch, so cook us some breakfast," orders Baldie. "Remember, one false move and we'll shackle you and lock you up again. If anyone comes to the front door this morning, let me deal with them. Your duty today is to go about with no clothes on and be our slave in every way. Understood?"

Moira nodded meekly, and later, the men guzzled more beer as Moira stood naked at the stove, frying their bacon and eggs. They ate breakfast together at the kitchen table like an odd nudist family.

"We're exhausted now," Baldie said. "So let us go to bed and sleep in a bit. Your job is to make us much more tired before we do that."

Back in the bedroom, Moira knelt on all fours on the carpet at the end of the bed. The men kneeled in front and back of her, their cocks again at the ready.

"Eat this," ordered Beardie and pushed the helmeted end of his dick to Moira's mouth as he roughly grabbed hair at the back of her head and pulled it towards his dick.

"Suck it!" he ordered. "Suck the cock until you get a mouthful!"

Moira has seen this threesome position in one or two of the erotic movies that belonged to her late husband, but she had always thought that it was a very contrived way, done just for show.

Baldie in the meantime grabbed hold of her ample behind and inserted his cock deep into her pussy. Again, secretly, this position actually very much turned Moira on. Two hard cocks were inside her, moving in and out in a very erotic way. The hard cocks', filling her mouth to bursting, was trickier to handle, tending to push sideways and too deep into her throat, gagging her.

Baldie thrust his thick dick inside her pussy at the rear end, so that she became some kind of a strange bridge between the three human beings; as the men were more sated, they take longer to gain their satisfaction. Again perversely, Moira enjoyed being her captors' mean to their ends. In fact, in her lonely routine and reclusive life at the dead end of a suburban world, what was happening to her was a real bonus, including even the painful spanking.

A hot stream filled her mouth so that she had to swallow quickly and carefully, while another discharge exploded inside her pussy. Well-timed, boys, she thought.

The spent men collapsed on the carpet at the end of the bed. Moira helped to pull the men up, one after another and tucked them in her big bed.

"Thanks, bitch, you have finally worn us out," says Baldie quietly.

"Have a bit of a rest, boys," Moira says, realizing that this is the first time in this whole ordeal that she has spoken. "It's not over yet, we have a long lazy Sunday ahead to spend having fun in bed."

"Aw, have pity on us," said Beardie, with a weak smile and his eyes half-closed.

"No way!" replied Moira, "Not after what you have done to me."

She crawled like a big fat cat from the end of the bed to squeeze in between the two men. As the men drape their arms over her, all three fell asleep, like one happy family.

In the late afternoon, Moira woke to some marvelous fondling of her body by strong hands from either side of her.

The men were feeling her body all over. A hand explored the folds of her cunt, gently for a change, and Beardie was feeling and squeezing the high full hills of her breasts.

"Shall we toss a coin again?" he asked

Baldie.

"No, I'll choose this time," said Moira. "It's your turn." She pointed to Baldie.

"Aw, why him?" whines Beardie.

"Because he didn't hit me with the wooden spoon."

On top of her, Baldie is amazingly still full of stamina, shoving in his hard and long cock and sending Moira to the edge time and time again, her pussy throbbing and gushing out streams of creamy white cum.

"Don't stop, please," Moira begged before screaming as she came.

"Well, boys, I think the fun is over," Moira finally said. "We'll get up in a while and I'll cook us some dinner. It's been some weekend, thanks boys."

"Margaret is arriving back tomorrow, isn't she, Bill?" Moira asked Beardie.

"Yes, tomorrow afternoon. I'll pick her up at the airport after work," said Bill.

"Jane should drive back tomorrow sometime as well, Jim?" Moira asked Baldie, a good neighbor who lives next door on the other side of her house. "I am sorry to see this end. It was great for me. But if you guys call me bitch or slut once more, I'll turn into one and do some damage to you!"

"Can I propose that we try to get your wives interested?" Moira added. "We'll make a good five some, or we may ask Dougie on the other side to join our group too. He's a lonely old sod."

"Sounds like a plan," Jim said and the three of them began to laugh.

AUTHOR'S NOTE

Readers: I want to expand a few of the stories to see where the characters can be explored further. If there are any of the stories that you would like to read more about again, I'd love to hear from you!

Visit my blog at www.charagladey.com

Join my newsletter for free exclusive previews
www.charagladey.com/in

Follow me on Twitter at
www.twitter.com/charagladey

Like my page on Facebook at
www.facebook.com/charagladey

Discover my books at major ebook retailers everywhere.

www.ingramcontent.com/pod-product-compliance
Lightning Source LLC
Chambersburg PA
CBHW032002170626
46807CB00006B/2615